I0780865

DIRE QUEEN

A.B. COHEN & JP RINDFLEISCH IX

This is a work of fiction. Names, characters, businesses, places, events, locales, and incidents are either the products of the author's imagination or used in a fictitious manner. Any resemblance to actual persons, living or dead, or actual events is purely coincidental.

Copyright © 2025 by A.B. Cohen & JP Rindfleisch IX

All rights reserved.

No part of this book may be reproduced in any form or by any electronic or mechanical means, including information storage and retrieval systems, without written permission from the author, except for the use of brief quotations in a book review.

Cover design by Getcovers.com

To Raquel & Josh.
For always being there.

Tree of Life

Divine One
Keter
Holy
Timekeeper
Binah
Time
Traveler
Chochmah
Space
Elemental
Gevurah
Nature
Lover
Chesed
Heal
Seer
Tiferet
Vision
Invulnerable
Netzach
Sheild
Pacifist
Hod
Hold
Bonded
Yesod
Link
Warrior
Malchut
Push

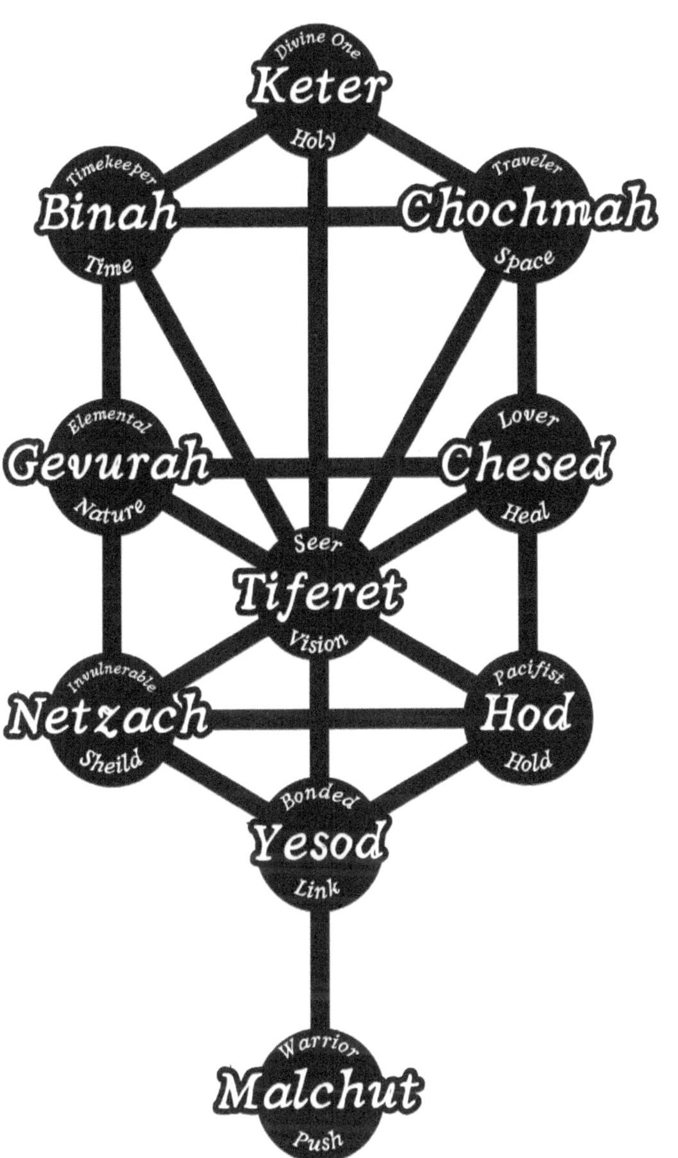

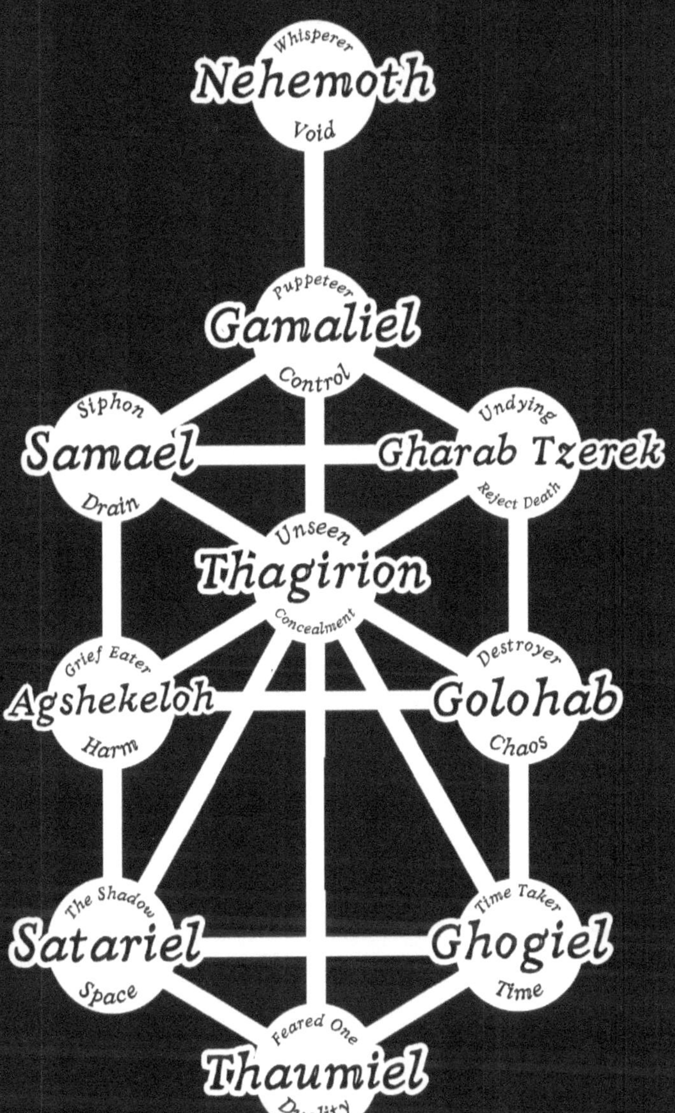

Tree of Death

The Infinity Board

 King

 White Queen

 Black Queen

 White Rook / Sage

 Black Rook

 White Bishop

 White Knight

 Black Bishop

 Black Knight

 White Pawn

 Black Pawn

 Square

CHAPTER 1
WAR HERO

"War hero."

The words made Leah's skin crawl as she stood at the edge of the Mystic camp, letting the cold winter wind sting her cheeks. She traced the scar on her shoulder where Legion had nearly torn her apart, trying to ignore the whispers that seemed to follow her everywhere now. Survivor. Savior. Even alone, she couldn't escape them—the constant murmurs of victories she didn't want and sacrifices she wished she could forget.

Gabe's arms around her on the marble steps of Maimonides Academy. How his ashy hair caught the sunlight. His final words as he—

Leah jerked her hand away from the scar. She was a war hero now, whatever that meant. And war heroes didn't cry, even when the weight of a thousand desperate hopes pressed down on their shoulders.

"Black Knight Ackerman?"

The deep voice brought Leah back. *Black Knight Ackerman.* She'd nearly forgotten she'd been promoted, alongside Sarah and Isaac, after Legion's attack. It wasn't ceremonious, just a pat on the shoulder as they filled the loss the Infinity Board suffered.

Leah quickly brushed away a tear that had escaped, then turned to find Ricky standing there, nearly as tall as herself. His messy black hair fell across his acne-covered forehead, and the shadow of a mustache was visible only at the corners of his lips. Despite his bulk from years of sports, he shifted his weight uncertainly.

Leah smiled, trying to soften her expression and hide her sadness. "Ricky, I've told you that you can call me Leah or Knight Ackerman if you must. I don't call any of you Squares."

Ricky looked down, his cheeks flushing. "Oh, right. I'm sorry, Black Knight—I mean Leah."

Leah stifled a chuckle, remembering how intimidating it had been to approach Alma with a question. Was she truly as imposing as her former mentor?

"We wanted to ask you about what happened... back at headquarters," Ricky continued, his usual skepticism replaced by hesitation.

Leah took a sharp inhale. Her mind surged with memories of deafening explosions and her fellow Mystics' agonized screams. She pushed the images away, focusing on the present.

"We?" She glanced behind Ricky and saw the rest of her Squares grouped, watching them. Ashley bounced nervously, her green eyes wide. Beside her, Callum's gangly frame seemed to fold in on itself as he studied the ground, freckles mottling his pale face. As soon as they noticed her gaze, they scattered, looking elsewhere. All except two.

Zoe, the youngest and smallest, stayed partially hidden behind Ashley, while Jenna stood a few feet behind the group, her light brunette ponytail swaying slightly as she maintained her arms behind her back in a *Malchut* position, continuing the training as instructed. Despite her size, the girl's eyes held sorrow that few adults knew.

Leah exhaled slowly, rubbing her forehead. "Okay, fine. Gather around everyone. You too, Jenna."

The group rushed forward. Ashley practically dragged Zoe with her while Callum tried to shrink his tall frame as he joined them. Only Jenna took her time, approaching with measured steps.

"I'll address this once, understand?" Leah said. "I can't have you all getting distracted like this."

"Yes, Black Knight Ackerman!" The response came in a chorus of varying enthusiasm—Ashley's voice carrying over Callum's mumble while Jenna's lips barely moved.

Leah sighed at the title and nodded at Ricky. "You have questions about what? Legion?"

Ricky shifted his feet, his usual skepticism creeping back into his voice. "We know what they're telling us, but... we've heard rumors."

Leah frowned. "What rumors?"

Zoe peered around Ashley, her quiet voice carrying a tremor. "I heard Legion is ten feet tall! And that it can grow multiple arms!"

"I heard Legion went toe-to-toe with the Queens, and they couldn't defeat him," Ricky added, raising his eyebrow.

Ashley leaned forward. "I heard you fought Legion single-handedly. What was it like?"

Questions spilled out of them—Callum opening and closing his mouth without speaking, Zoe's eyes growing wider with each new rumor. Leah had to raise her hand for silence. She scanned the group, pausing on Jenna, who had her eyes fixed on a spot behind Leah. The weight of their expectations pressed down on her—Leah Ackerman, the White Pawn who had faced Legion and lived. A symbol that proved ranks didn't matter.

Leah swallowed hard, her throat dry. She knew what the Rooks and Queens wanted her to say. Keep morale high. Keep the details of what happened at headquarters vague. But it was all hollow, disconnected from reality.

"What they want me to say is that everything is being taken care of. They want me to tell you we're safe," Leah began. "They don't believe young Squares are ready for the truth. But I was where you were less than two years ago. I know you deserve the truth."

She paused, staring at each of them. Even Jenna had finally looked up, hanging on Leah's words.

"Two months ago, our headquarters were ambushed. We weren't prepared when Legion attacked," Leah continued. "He weaseled his way into our ranks, using our own against us. Pawns, Bishops, Knights, hell, even Rooks were possessed. They attacked, and—"

Her voice caught in her throat. The sickening crunch of bones breaking, the acrid smell of smoke and blood, Gabe's last words...

She closed her eyes and shook off the memories. "We lost many people that day. And many, including myself, faced Legion and lived."

"But you saved everyone with that... potion?" Ricky asked.

"Mandrake potion, yes," she said. "It didn't kill Legion, but it was enough to stop the fight."

Ashley frowned. "But if we hurt him so badly, why are we stuck here at the edge of Sekrè Fami? Why can't we leave here?"

"Three Queens were there that night, and it took a potion from the Druids to stop him. We are at this voodoo town because we need the rootworker's protective spells while we find out who's still possessed in our ranks," Leah explained.

"They don't want us here."

Everyone turned to Jenna.

Leah raised an eyebrow. "And how do you know that?"

Jenna clenched her jaw and shook her head.

"Our agreement with the people here is cordial at best. We're lucky they let us set up camp outside of town." She pursed her lips as she looked at Jenna. "None of you should be setting foot in town."

"Yes, Black Knight Ackerman!" They all said in unison.

After a moment, Leah stood up straight and placed her hands behind her back. "It's important to take care of each other, understand? Even the Infinity Board won't keep your secrets. Find a small circle you can trust, and play the game."

She paused, remembering her time back at the Outpost and the Academy. Compared to now, those times were simple, and she wished she could somehow go back. "Class dismissed. Go shower and get ready for dinner." As the others turned to leave, she added, "Jenna, a word."

The other Squares hurried back towards the camp while Jenna remained attentive, her posture rigid.

Leah crossed her arms, leaning in closer to the girl. "So, you've been going into town again?"

Jenna remained silent.

"Jenna, you're lucky I caught you the first time," Leah said, doing her best to sound stern. "If any other Knight, or a Rook, sees you, then—"

"So, what if I did?" Jenna interrupted, still eying the ground. "We shouldn't be stuck out here."

Leah crossed her arms. "You're not even bonded to a mentor. If a faction gets hold of you..."

Jenna finally looked up, her eyes blazing. "Why do you care? Just leave me alone!"

Leah recognized those eyes. The same look she'd given

herself in the mirror plenty of times. The eyes of someone carrying too much on their shoulders. Eyes of a survivor.

"Jenna, I know what it's like," Leah whispered.

"No, you don't." Jenna's voice was barely above a whisper.

"Legion killed almost all of my squad. I've lost family, friends... loves." Leah reached out, placing a hand on Jenna's shoulder, but the girl shoved it off.

"Where was the Infinity Board when my outpost got attacked?" Jenna spat. "Where were you?"

The words cut Leah like a knife. She clenched her jaw, fighting to maintain her composure. If she'd known about the attack on the outpost, she would have been there in a heartbeat. She would have been at every single attack. But they kept it from her because they needed their supposed "war hero" safe.

Leah steeled herself. "You're dismissed, Square."

Leah watched Jenna disappear between the tents, her heart heavy. The girl's anger was justified but didn't make it any easier. She took a deep breath, trying to center herself.

"Rough session?"

Sarah's voice cut through Leah's thoughts. She turned to see her friend, with her hair pulled back into a single afro puff, standing next to Isaac, with his blond hair cut short. They approached, wearing the same black cloaks as her, billowing in the icy wind. Sarah wore the same Knight insignia on hers, while Isaac sported a Bishop. Despite everything, a small smile tugged at her lips.

"You have no idea," Leah sighed, grateful for the distraction.

Isaac gave a half-smile and shook his head. "I don't blame her. Her Outpost was horrific when we got there. We tried to clean up most of it before pulling her up from the floorboards of the basement. Didn't help her shock, though."

"I've tried to give her space." Leah watched as Jenna disappeared behind one of the green tents. "But she channels her anger towards me and any other leader in the Infinity Board. I even tried talking to her about the Queen's Gambit, but she won't listen."

Sarah patted Leah on the back. "Don't beat yourself up. Give her time. Remember how you first were at the outpost?"

"I wasn't that bad!" Leah placed a hand dramatically on her chest.

Isaac smirked. "Right, because sending Paige flying across the training field and breaking her arm was *totally* normal."

"Hey, I was defending your ass," Leah retorted, and they all burst into laughter.

For a moment, they were back to how things were, in those moments of calm and peace that Leah hadn't had in months.

As their laughter subsided, Sarah paused. "Do you think she's okay?"

"Who?" Isaac asked.

"Paige."

Leah glanced up at the cloudy sky. "I hope so. I'm just glad we didn't find her among the sacrificed. Maybe we can hope she's off somewhere with other chimeras in Europe or somewhere else away from all this."

"That would be nice," Sarah said.

After a moment, Leah looked back at her friends. "Have any news for me?"

Sarah punched Issac's shoulder and grinned. "Well, this guy finally got us some good news. He overheard plans for a meeting tonight with the Rooks and Queens."

"Nice!" Leah smiled. "How'd you manage that?"

Isaac rubbed his arm. "We were back at the academy in Iowa. Supposedly, demons were squatting there, so we wanted to root them out and find out if any of them were tracking us." He looked around and lowered his voice. "Zafirah was talking to Jan Xie in the next room. I don't think she thought anyone could hear her, but I heard they were meeting Helen, Micah, and the other Sages here tonight."

Leah crossed her arms. "Perfect. I'll use *Thagirion* to slip past the guards, then."

A loud snap from the forest sounded behind them, and they all looked toward the empty woods.

"These woods are creepy," Sarah said, shivering as her eyes blazed yellow.

"We fight demons, but the woods get you?" Isaac joked.

Sarah readied another punch to Isaac's arm, but he jumped out of the way, racing toward the camp. "Too slow!"

Leah laughed and followed them back toward camp, dead leaves crunching beneath their feet.

"You'd think our 'war hero' would get front-row seats to meetings," Sarah said.

"Can you please stop calling me that?" Leah groaned.

Sarah slowed and walked beside Leah, draping an arm over her shoulders. "Sorry. It's just that they keep calling you that, but then you're stuck here training Squares while they stick us on the front lines. None of it makes sense."

Leah sighed. "It's all part of the game. Make a symbol for people to look up to so they fight. I just wish it wasn't me. Trust me, I'd rather be out there with you guys."

As they reached the camp's border, they walked past the outer tents, all black with the insignias of Bishops who monitored the perimeter. Even with the rootworker's spell work, the fallout from the attack on headquarters left many in the Infinity Board questioning who to trust.

As they made their way through, several Mystics popped their heads out of tents while others simply stopped to stare.

"Wow, so they don't even hide the gawking now." Sarah glared at a group of young Mystics.

"It's only gotten worse, too," Leah said. "Now that news of what happened with the Queen's Gambit was declassified."

With her two friends flanking her, it was easier for Leah to endure the attention, even if everyone staring at her made her stomach churn. As they passed, a cluster of young Squares huddled near the path, snippets of their excited whispers carried on the wind.

"...suck the life out of demons..."

"...fought Legion herself..."

Leah caught sight of a blond girl, no older than thirteen, gesturing to her friend with braces, their eyes wide as they stared at her. She clenched her jaw, her eyes fixed on the ground as she pulled up the hood of her cloak.

"Ignore them," Isaac whispered, his voice barely audible. "It'll all blow over."

Leah nodded, then cleared her throat. "Either of you heard anything about Nykima?"

Isaac shook his head.

Sarah exhaled and looked off toward the houses in Sekrè Fami. "Nothing since they sent her back."

"It's not right. Nykima should be the war hero. Not me," Leah said.

"They had to blame someone," Sarah said. "Now that she's back in there, I haven't heard a peep."

Isaac looked over towards the small brick buildings across the other side of the camp where Sekrè Fami began.

"How much longer do you think the Queen's plan on keeping us separated from this voodoo town like this?"

"We've been here a month," Leah grumbled, pulling her cloak close. "They better figure something out because I'm getting tired of these tents. And it doesn't help that the Queens get to stay in actual houses."

Sarah nodded toward one of the brick walls, with bright purple graffiti that read *We Remember 1891.* "With all the faction nonsense they're having, it might not be a good time to let us in any way."

"But we have treaties," Leah muttered. "And now that Nykima is with their so-called Voodoo Queen, then I don't know what is taking them so long. It's just another bureaucracy. No better than the Infinity Board."

They entered their canvas tent and took off their cloaks. Inside, it was spacious, with a battery and a heater keeping it warm.

Leah passed by Isaac's bed, with a book on top that read "Voodoo Magic, Logic and Practical Uses" next to his walkie-talkie, which he had for reconnaissance missions. She reached the corner and stretched her body on her squeaky bed. Her shoulder and ribs mostly healed from the battle at headquarters, although the exhaustion persisted. After all, *Chesed* could only do so much.

As Leah drifted off, the faint crackle of static filled her ears—a sound that had haunted her since Legion's attack.

CHAPTER 2

WE REMEMBER 1891

As she stepped into the first layer of the Astral, Leah's skin prickled. The familiar chill of *Thagirion* settled over her, not quite cold but lacking warmth. Sounds muffled, and the world took on a sickly yellow tinge as if viewed through an old film. She paused at the entrance of her tent, scanning the landscape.

"You don't need me to come with you?"

Leah turned, finding the ghostly boy Tom hovering near her bed. His form flickered, its edges blurring into the shadows. She eyed the black tome on her bedside table. It was the book his spirit was bound to, which she had carried since headquarters.

"No," Leah said, catching her breath after being startled. "It's best if you stay back," Leah said. "If I get caught, I don't want them to know about you."

Tom's shoulders slumped. "Oh, okay."

Leah felt a pang of guilt. She crouched beside him, trying to meet his gaze.

"I know you haven't been able to do much," she said. "The Infinity Board has me on a short leash. They want to keep their precious 'war hero' safe and sound. But I still remember my promise. As soon as we locate Anat, I'll get you to her, okay?"

Tom smiled up at her, a glimmer of hope in his eyes. Leah returned the smile, though she didn't know if it was a promise she could keep.

She stood, adjusting her cloak, and stepped out of the tent. The camp sprawled before her, a mix of torn and decayed tents and forest in the eerie Astral light. Leah moved slowly, knowing her steps could still be heard from anyone on the physical side.

She heard muffled sounds as she passed a repurposed brick warehouse now serving as their cafeteria. Two bishops were entering, trailing smoke in the astral realm as their white cloaks gleamed. Leah pressed herself against the building's cold surface, waiting for them to pass.

Lovely night-time stroll, Asmodeus's voice drawled in her mind.

"Look who's up," Leah muttered, feeling the demon stir inside her.

The training with your Squares is dull at best. And with this little excursion of yours, I figured I should save my strength.

"It's not that bad," Leah said, crossing an empty street lined with abandoned storefronts and weathered houses. "Training the new Mystics is worth it if I can't be out of the front lines."

Training kids for war? Oh yeah, that sounds lovely. Asmodeus laughed.

"Better than leaving them with nothing while demons keep attacking," Leah said. "They have targets on their backs. Might as well make sure they can defend themselves."

Whatever you say.

Leah brushed off the demon's words, focusing on the task at hand. She approached an intersection, spotting two

Mystics in white cloaks guarding a small Victorian house. Its once-pristine pink pastel paint had chipped away, revealing blackened wood underneath. The windows on the second floor were boarded up, making it look like nearly all the other homes in this district.

A quick *Tiferet* inspection revealed no one inside yet. Leah's heartbeat quickened. She was early—the meeting hadn't started. And now came the tricky part: getting in undetected.

Leah scanned her surroundings, counting six cloaked figures patrolling the area. In the astral, a hole in the side of the house offered her a glimpse of the living room within. Documents spread across a table, while maps and posters adorned the walls. But she couldn't just crawl through. It was too cramped—she'd be spotted in an instant.

Then, she saw a hole near the roof, right next to a tree, close enough for her to reach.

This first layer has its perks, Asmodeus mused. *With all this rot free for you to move through.*

Leah couldn't argue with that. She crept around the house, reaching the tallest tree and climbing it, her movements slow and deliberate to minimize noise. Stretching her arm, she grasped the edge of the roof and hauled herself up, rolling through the hole.

A Mystic below turned, his eyes flashing yellow as he scanned the rooftop. Leah froze, pressing herself flat against the weathered shingles. Her heart thumped as she held her breath. After an agonizing moment, the Mystic's eyes dimmed, and he resumed his patrol.

The roof creaked beneath her weight as Leah crept toward the hole. Her heart hammered against her ribs as she eased herself down, praying the rotted wood wouldn't give way. She landed in what must have once been an attic, now little more than a hollow shell of decay. A sickly yellow glow seeped up through the floorboards, casting strange shadows as she picked her way toward the ancient stairs.

At the bottom, she took a left, following the light spilling from the living room. Newspapers were scattered across the dining table, their headlines circled in red ink:

UNEXPLAINED FIRE KILLS 77, 41 OF THEM CHILDREN
GAS LEAK CAUSES MASSIVE FIRE IN GHOST TOWN

Leah's stomach churned as she flipped through the articles detailing similar tragedies.

Looks like the attacks have increased, Asmodeus said, his voice uncharacteristically somber.

"Yeah," Leah whispered, her throat tight. "It's been over a month, and we still haven't located and evacuated all the Mystics. I'm not sure we ever will at this point."

All those locations were consumed in the fire, and you Mystics love your secrets. I'm surprised you've saved as many as you did.

Leah nodded, moving to examine a large U.S. map hanging on the wall behind the long table. Red and green pins dotted its surface, connected by a red string that formed an unsettling, asymmetrical symbol across the eastern United States. Near the crescent center, a black pin marked a spot just outside Washington D.C. in Shenandoah National Park.

Leah shivered. "That's HQ."

She remembered a version of this map hanging in Constance's office. The green pins, she recalled, represented human sacrifices scattered across the country. The red pins were chimera sacrifices, far fewer in number, their locations forming a deliberate path to create the symbol.

This was how Legion broke through the Astral Layers and brought his army down on us, Asmodeus said.

"Does that symbol look familiar to you?" Leah asked, leaning closer to the map. "I don't think I've seen that before."

It's not that specific one, no. But it looks similar to the ones we've used back in The Valley. The green means nothing to me, though. They don't have any pattern or logic.

Leah frowned. "So, it's possible the only sacrifices that mattered were Chimeras? Why? And why all those human sacrifices?"

Images of the countless corpses they'd found during the Queen's Gambit operation flashed through her mind. Nightmares that haunted her.

Knowing Legion, Asmodeus started. *These were likely decoys. What better way to pull the Infinity Board's attention than to sacrifice people without a pattern while doing the actual work on creatures Mystics care little about?*

Anger built in Leah's chest, energy stirring like a restless snake. All those lives lost, just to distract...

The muffled sound of a door opening snapped Leah back to reality. She whirled around, crouching behind an old white couch near the hole in the wall. Pressed against its musty fabric, she held her breath as footsteps approached.

Black Queen Helen entered first, followed by White Queen Micah and the Sages Nick, Eli, and Zafirah. Leah peered over the couch, her eyes wide. She hadn't seen the Queens since the attack on HQ. The toll of the past month was evident on their faces.

The sight of Micah made Leah's breath catch. His commanding presence she remembered was gone—in his place was a man worn thin by weeks of crisis, silver threading through his hair. But Helen... Leah had to hold back a gasp. The Black Queen's skin had taken on a sickly color, almost green in the dim light. Every movement seemed to cost her as she eased herself into a chair, wincing as she did.

"Gods, it's freezing in here," Nick muttered, rubbing his hands together.

Eli's paused, sweeping over the room. Leah's heart thundered so loud in her chest she was certain he'd hear it when his gaze settled on her hiding spot. She pressed herself deeper into shadow, hardly daring to breathe. One heartbeat. Two. Then the creak of a chair as he finally sat.

"The heater's probably malfunctioning again," Zafirah said, settling beside Micah. Unlike the others, she seemed unbothered by the chill, dressed in a simple white T-shirt and shorts. "Perfect for me. I'm so hot," she added, fanning herself.

"I don't envy the *Gevurah* effect on you," Nick muttered, shaking his head. He walked to the hallway, checking the thermostat. "It says it's on. Maybe it just takes some time?"

As the group settled, a White Bishop entered, setting up a laptop and speakers at the center of the table before hurrying out.

"Can everyone hear me?" A familiar voice crackled through the speakers.

"Yes, Jan," Micah replied. "Are Yuki and Desmond with you?"

"We are," Desmond's deep voice confirmed.

Micah leaned forward, his fingers interlaced on the table. "Okay, let's go over our numbers."

Black Queen Jan Xie cleared her throat. "We've located and evacuated thirty-seven percent of our Outpost members and forty-two percent of our Academy members. Many fell within the first week of the attack, but we're still tracking survivors." Her voice tightened. "We've recovered seven Squares, twelve Knights, eighteen Bishops, and one Rook. All were cleared of possession and sent to different safe houses. Do you have room there for any additional Mystics?"

"Bad idea," Helen said, shaking her head. She winced, grabbing onto her neck. "Madeline is still struggling with one faction here. They call themselves the 1891. Bringing in more Mystics now would just add more fuel to the fire."

"Fine," Jan said sharply. "I'll find somewhere else for them then. But we have already lost three safe houses. They'll be sitting ducks, just like the rest of them, until we can get Madeline to let us in. That town is the safest place we have."

"I know. We're trying," Micah said, clenching his fist. "It's not that simple."

"People are dying," Jan snapped. "Get it done."

Micah shifted uncomfortably in his chair before replying, "I hear you, Jan. We'll work harder. Do what you do best for now, and keep them hidden."

After a moment of silence, Helen asked, "What's the situation abroad?"

"We are—" Jan's words suddenly drowned out by a burst of harsh static.

Leah winced, covering her ears, but to her surprise, no one else in the room reacted to the noise. After a few agonizing seconds, Jan's voice returned mid-sentence.

"...South Africa and Zimbabwe have both been affected as well. We're moving pieces around to relocate everyone, but it isn't looking good."

Leah frowned, looking to the others in the room for any reaction to that static she'd heard. A flicker of movement caught her eye. She stood, her breath catching in her throat, as she saw a translucent head emerging from the wall behind Helen. It wasn't an Astral creature—its features were too human, but it was too faded, almost like it was made of smoke.

That's no creature, Asmodeus said. *Looks like an essence.*

Leah frowned, keeping still as the figure pulled more of itself through the wall. It was some kind of human, but it was barely there. "Essence?" she whispered.

"The Druids have moved down south," Micah said. "However, Legion's demons seem to be fixated only on Mystics for now."

Helen's lips thinned into a tight line. "Any intel on Legion, Jan?"

"No. We've had no reports since the attack on HQ. Whatever your girl did to him must have hurt him good. No reports of Sandeep or Nona either." Jan's sigh crackled through the speakers. "Legion is probably using Nona to predict our moves and stay hidden. That's my current theory."

The essence was far too focused on the group to see Leah. She raised her head higher, invoking *Tiferet*. The world sharpened into focus, and the essence took shape. It was a man, bald, with dark coppery skin.

Suddenly, the man turned, locking eyes with Leah. He jumped, vanishing back into the wall.

"What the...?" Leah whispered.

Without thinking, Leah sprung from her hiding place and darted through the hole in the wall. She glimpsed the essence floating away down the street.

Why are we chasing ghosts? Asmodeus asked.

"Because I don't think that's a ghost," Leah said, concentrating her energy. She executed a *Malchut* push, propelling herself forward in a burst of speed.

She raced after the essence, which took sharp turns between intersections in Sekrè Fami, evading her. But she kept pace, using the brick walls to push off and maintain her momentum. She was closing the gap when the essence ducked into a tight alley.

A burst of static screamed in Leah's ears, catching her off balance and causing her to stumble. She clutched her head, looking wildly for the source as the white noise grew louder and louder. A nearby electronics store flashed TV screens of static.

"Come... Me..." a voice shouted through the noise.

Leah squeezed her eyes shut, the sound too painful and too loud. In her disorientation, she dropped *Thagirion*, the cold bricks forming beneath her.

The static ring faded away, replaced by the sound of distant traffic. The electronic store contained televisions with screens playing a nature documentary.

As she gathered her bearings, her gaze fell on fresh graffiti adorning one of the alley's brick walls:

We Remember 1891

Racing footsteps pulled her from the graffiti to see five young men in hoodies closing in on her position.

"Look, it was a Mystic!" one of them shouted. He was a young bald man who looked oddly familiar. He was also the only one not wearing a small, strange doll around his neck.

"Get her before she gets away," another snapped.

Leah's mind raced. She was outnumbered. Worse, she was nowhere near the Mystic camp. She rose to her feet, muscles tensed, readying for a fight.

Two men, wearing black hoodies with skull bandanas covering the lower half of their faces, stepped forward. Leah braced herself for an attack, but they split off, each pulling a spray can from their pockets. To her bewilderment, they painted a circle on the ground around her in no time while muttering words under their breath.

Leah called her energy, not interested in whatever ritual they were trying to capture her in. She sent out a *Malchut* push aimed squarely at the chest of the nearest guy. But, instead of throwing him from her, an energy peeled off him for a moment, as if his spirit detached for a moment before snapping back into place. He looked at her and grinned.

The two men finished the circle of red paint and backed away. As they did, the energy in Leah's fists drained away.

"What the hell?" she whispered, shaking her hands, willing the energy to return.

The man who'd shouted orders stepped forward, grinning as he reached the edge of the circle. "Looks like we caught ourselves a Mystic breaking the treaty, boys."

"I don't want any trouble," Leah called out, her voice steady despite her racing heart. The street out of the alley remained empty—of course, they'd chosen this moment when no one else was around to witness.

The leader laughed. "A Mystic saying they don't want trouble? That's rich." In the dim light, Leah could see the hatred on his face. "Your kind brings nothing *but* trouble. And now little Mystics like you walk our streets like you own them?"

Leah eyed the tiny Voodoo dolls hanging from leather cords around their necks—all except for the one she'd attacked, who was hastily replacing his.

"I... I got lost," She said, forcing her voice to remain calm while frantically trying to call on her energy. Nothing. The circle had cut her off entirely from the Tree of Life. "I'll leave. I'll go back to camp."

You know they won't let us go that easily, Asmodeus whispered in her mind.

The leader's expression darkened as he pulled a pair of brass knuckles onto his fingers. "A Mystic's word?" He spat on the ground. "Our forefathers trusted Mystics, which got them six feet under." He snarled as he eyed her. "We remember. We remember for them."

He stepped over the line and swiftly punched her in the side, doubling Leah over. Pain seared through her as they kicked and punched. She called on *Malchut*, trying to push them away, but her energy peeled off them harmlessly. Then she noticed it: tiny voodoo dolls hanging from leather cords around their necks that glowed for a moment.

She curled up on the ground, trying to defend herself, but each punch and kick felt like it carried the strength of three men. She reached up through the haze of pain and yanked a talisman free before curling back into a ball.

Is this really how it ends? Leah thought, her bones groaning and tasting blood in her mouth. *Not protecting others, but beaten in an alley?*

An energy formed in her throat, twisting around her vocal cords, waiting for her to speak. "Stop!" she screamed, the energy tearing through her.

The kicks stopped for a moment. Leah looked up to see the five men dazed and backing away. But before she could react, four of them shook their malaise free. The leader, his neck now bare of the talisman, stumbled backward, his eyes wide with fear as he realized his protection was gone.

One of the men kicked her side, sending white-hot agony through her. The world fell away, and suddenly, she was in a vast, dark space, ankle-deep in water.

Two flames burned before her—one blue-turquoise, the other green-black, their light pulsing in rhythm with each blow her physical body received.

Asmodeus appeared next to her, drawn to the flames like a moth. Whispers echoed out from the dark, not threatening like *Nehemoth*, but a calling, urging her to take the fire.

Asmodeus circled the green flame, his starry eyes gleaming. Then, he grabbed the fire and voice echoed in her mind; *Satariel.*

Power formed in Leah, dulling the physical pain she felt in her physical body. She snapped her eyes open, seeing double vision. One was still lying on the ground, fending off kicks.

But the other stood outside the circle, staring at the men, kicking a poor, defenseless girl.

This is power. I can't hold it. Get them. Now! Asmodeus's voice screamed in her mind.

Leah reached out to *Malchut*, feeling it build in the version of her that stood outside the circle. She sent a horizontal wave of force, throwing her attackers off her crumpled form.

She looked up at herself, the one standing outside the circle. Her other self smiled, wincing as she held her side, then vanished into dark mist.

As the men groaned behind her, Leah pushed herself up, stumbling out of the circle. She didn't have time to figure out what the hell just happened. She had to run.

CHAPTER 3
INFUSED MAGIC

Leah stumbled out of the alley, her body aching, one of her ribs certainly on the verge of cracking. She heard the men behind her scrambling to their feet and racing after her. They would reach her any second now. She called on her energy, but it slipped through her fingers like water. She was drained.

Suddenly, the footsteps stopped, and she risked a glance. They were frozen in mid-chase, eyes trained on her. She backed into a wall, looking up and down the alley for who or what stopped them.

"This is a surprise," drawled a familiar Scottish accent.

Jaime McMillan, the Black Rook who she'd met at headquarters, turned out from the shadows behind her attackers. He sauntered past them, pulling one of the voodoo necklaces free and eyeing it before tossing it aside.

"You sure cause a lot of trouble," Jaime mused, his words slightly slurred. "Why did you—"

A deep, bronchial cough cut him off. The man grabbed his shoulder, squeezing hard as he regained his composure. Leah winced, remembering the dark marks on his neck hidden behind his white scarf. The markings of his shifter curse. He pulled out a flask and took a quick swig. Throughout this all, he kept the middle finger of his left hand pressed to the top of his index finger, the more advanced technique of *Hod* that kept the men frozen.

"Apologies," Jaime cleared his throat. "Where was I? Ah, yes." He glared at the young men, whose faces were now turning a shade of purple. "You gentlemen feel good about yourselves? Hmm? Cornering a fourteen-year-old?"

"I'm seventeen," Leah corrected, her voice raw. She touched her throat, surprised by the pain.

Jaime turned to her, eyebrows raised. "Really?" He shrugged and continued, "Well, you five sure as hell are lucky. Guaranteed if you got her again, that one would have made sure you left this alley in body bags."

"Ba...st...ard," the leader managed through gritted teeth.

Jaime moved closer, almost nose to nose with the man. He slipped down the handkerchief covering the attacker's face.

"So, you're the ringleader." Jaime's voice dropped low. "I'm going to let this little tussle slide since this Mystic clearly stepped out of bounds. However, if you ever lay a finger on a Mystic again, you and your friends are dead, you hear me?"

The man simply glared back at Jaime, refusing to even try to speak.

After a few moments of silence, Jaime gave the man two soft slaps on the face. "Good boy."

He turned back to Leah, unwinding his fingers. The five men collapsed to the ground, gasping for air.

"Can you walk?" Jaime asked, gripping Leah's shoulder.

She clutched her side, pain searing her chest. She shook her head. Jaime's eyes flashed yellow as he looked her up and down before his gaze snapped back to the leader on the ground. In two quick strides, Jamie snatched the brass knuckles from the man's hand.

"These are coming with us," Jaime growled. He returned to Leah, holding out a hand. "Here, let me help."

Warm energy flowed from Jaime's hands as he hovered them over Leah. The pain receded to a dull ache, and the warmth flowed into her throat, soothing the rawness.

"Better?" Jaime asked.

Leah rotated her hip slowly. "Yes, thanks." She pushed herself up. "What are those?"

Jaime wrapped her arm around her shoulder, and they walked out into the street. He held up the brass knuckles, turning them over. "They're infused with magic. Not strong, but enough to take a toll."

"More so than regular brass knuckles?" Leah grabbed them and looked at the chipped brass.

"I've seen better ones, but the magic acts like an invisible blade, tearing up your insides. You probably didn't even know you were bleeding out."

"I... did not," Leah breathed, a hand running along her side. "Well, thank you for being there."

Amber streetlights illuminated their path as they walked back toward camp. Leah lost herself in thought, regaining her strength the longer they walked.

"So," Jaime's voice cut through her thoughts, "what were you doing in that alley, so far from camp?"

Leah bit her lip, considering her options. "What were *you* doing?"

"Ah," Jaime grinned. "I asked you first."

She took in a breath, then said. "I... I was spying on the meeting between the Queen and Sages. I saw something, an essence, and chased it down. But then..."

Jaime eyed her. "Then what?"

Leah shook her head. "I don't know. There was a loud

static noise, and I dropped my *Thagirion*. That's when those guys found me."

"I see." Jaime nodded slowly. "Well, you're lucky I found you in time."

Leah looked down, heat rising to her cheeks. "Thank you…"

Jaime waved her off again. "Don't mention it. We're even now."

Leah frowned. Jaime caught her eye and clarified, "You saved all of us from that attack. You are a hero."

"Oh, not you, too…" Leah groaned.

Jaime's laugh echoed off the empty street. He took out his flask and took another sip. "I understand the feeling. Watching them parade my son around as their war hero after the shifters took him…" He shook his head bitterly. "It changes you."

Leah's heart sank. "I'm sorry."

"Not your fault, lass," Jaime sighed. "Tell me, why do you hate it? Nearly everyone else I know would love the special treatment."

Leah paused, collecting her thoughts before saying, "I'm a hero born from a battle we lost. I wasn't quick enough, too obsessed, thinking you were possessed and trying to undermine everything. Had I done more, had I stopped to think, maybe so many wouldn't have died. I can't keep standing in front of everyone and act like I'm proud when all I feel is shame."

Jaime reached under his cloak and handed Leah his metal flask. "Here, if they want to call you a war hero, then you deserve a swig of this."

She hesitated but took it, unscrewing the top and smelling a sharp tang of caramel and wood smoke. She looked at him, eyeing the spot under his scarf. "But, your—"

"Oh no, this isn't potion, just regular scotch," Jaime assured her. "Haven't been able to take that since we left HQ."

Leah took a sip. The liquid spread across her mouth like fire, first sweet, then smoky as she swallowed, warming her throat and belly. She coughed, unable to hold back the burning sensation.

"Good stuff, isn't it?" Jaime asked.

Leah cleared her throat, handing the flask back to him. "Strong might be a better word."

Jaime chuckled, taking a swig. "Suit yourself."

As they walked, the sounds of music grew louder. They passed by a parade, slipping through alleys before entering another empty street.

"I'm sorry about Gabe," Jaime said. "I know he was special to you."

Leah exhaled, a pain in her heart digging in as she saw his face in her mind. "He was."

"It's not easy. And I know it's not the same, but them using my son as their idol for battle... it made me sick. That's you now, a symbol for them to use. And we might have lost, but without what you did, we would have lost more. You gave people hope when they needed it."

They emerged onto a wide street bustling with people and lined with lively bars. Neon lights flashed, and the air was thick with the scent of alcohol and fried food.

"Ah, this is more like it," Jaime said. He adjusted his white scarf and continued walking.

Leah hurried to catch up. "Wait, weren't we trying to avoid crowds?"

Jaime shook his head. "Not here. This is one of Madeline's districts. We're safe here as long as you're with me."

Leah frowned. "But what were you doing in the 1891 district, anyway?"

Jaime shrugged. "There's a quieter bar there."

"Right," Leah said, confident he wouldn't tell her anymore if she pressed. Instead, she asked, "Why do they call themselves the 1891? Didn't the Treaty of Lyon start in 1892? That's what Alma taught me."

Jaime nodded, slowing his pace toward the bar. "Aye, but they see 1891 as their downfall when Augustin Delva, a leader of the resistance, was assassinated. He'd united all the rootworkers, encouraging them to use their magic freely and out in the open. The Infinity Board saw him as a threat and neutralized him."

Leah narrowed her eyes. "Wait, what? They killed him? Why?"

He paused, watching a group of laughing people stumble out of a nearby bar. "Well, that's the crux of it, isn't it? They would say he was unifying them, but Mystics reports at the time suggested he was delving into some of the darkest magic, killing anyone who stood in the way of progress. They might have been a unified front, but at what cost?"

They passed by a loud bar filled with people dancing and laughing. Leah considered his words, thinking of everything that's happened to her. Even now, with Asmodeus inside her, she understood how easy it would be to cross that line in the name of progress.

"Do you think he was as evil as they say?" she asked Jaime.

"Augustin was complicated. I have a copy of an unofficial biography from his grandkids. Even they said when he delved into the tree of death, it only brought more death. It's like the old saying: 'Dark magic begets dark magic.'"

"I've heard that before!" Leah exclaimed.

"I'm sure you have." Jaime laughed before turning serious again. "In the end, they want balance just as much as we do, but they need the tip of the scales to see it. Most of them want peace now."

"You really think that?" Leah asked as they neared the end of the road, the Infinity Board camp coming into view.

Jaime nodded confidently. "I do, lass. Especially with Legion coming into power. Madeline and others like her know we need balance again." They stopped at the edge of camp. "Well, here you are, safe and sound."

"Uh, thanks." Leah scratched the back of her head.

"Of course," Jaime replied. "But I still need to report this, you know?"

"What? Why?" Leah asked, eyes wide.

"I'm kidding." Jaime chuckled. "You're a Black Knight, not a Pawn. Just be sure to hide that bruise on your cheek. Don't want anyone asking questions, yeah?"

"Yeah," Leah said, steeling herself as she broke free from Jaime and back to camp.

CHAPTER 4

THE TWO FLAMES

The metallic tang of blood still coated her tongue from the fight as Leah stepped into the tent. Sarah and Isaac sprang up from their beds, eyes wide in the dim glow of the single bulb, like two owls in the dark.

"Where have you been?" Sarah asked, then narrowed her eyes. "Is that a bruise?"

Leah's fingers grazed her cheek, a wince escaping her. "It's nothing. Just... ran into some complications."

Isaac took a step forward. "Complications? Leah, you look like you've been through hell."

She sank onto her squeaky bed, exhaustion seeping into her bones. "You could say that. I... I need to tell you something. Both of you."

Sarah and Isaac frowned, then joined her on either side. Sarah nudged Leah's shoulder. "What is it?"

Leah took a deep breath, the words tumbling out in a rush. She told them about eavesdropping on the Queens' meeting, the mysterious essence she'd chased, the static that had overwhelmed her senses, and the attack by the 1891 faction. Sarah's fists balled up with each revelation while Isaac's frown deepened.

"So, they're spying on the Queens?" Isaac asked, looking around the corners of the tent. "That's... concerning."

Sarah leaned forward, her eyes blazing. "Forget that. Those bastards attacked you! We should—"

"We should what?" Leah cut in, her voice sharp. "Start a war with the locals? That's exactly what they want."

Isaac cleared his throat. "But the static thing, that doesn't make sense. There's nothing in the books I've been studying about that."

Sarah rolled her eyes. "Not everything's going to be in your books, Isaac."

"No, but it explains the logic behind their magic," Isaac pressed on, tapping the cover of 'Voodoo Magic, Theory and Practical Uses.' "They rely heavily on the Trees to create objects like Voodoo dolls, talismans, and weapons. Plus, they use specific powders for different purposes, like the defensive circle we put together at HQ or the powder we used on those guards. This static attack doesn't follow that pattern."

Leah frowned, her mind racing. "So what? You're suggesting they have someone or something else working for them?"

"I don't know," Isaac said. "But that can't be good."

Sarah's voice cut through the silence. "Hey. You okay? And don't give me that 'I'm fine' bullshit."

Leah slumped onto her cot, running a hand through her hair. "No. I always feel a step behind. It doesn't help that the Queens won't tell me anything either. It's like they only want their precious war hero when it's convenient."

"Well, you've got us," Isaac said. His shoulder pressed against hers.

The simple truth of it burned in her throat. Leah could

only nod, afraid that if she spoke, everything she'd been holding back would come spilling out.

Sarah bounced to her feet, pacing their cramped tent. "Well, if something out there can take down our mighty hero—" she flashed Leah a quick, crooked smile "—then we've got bigger problems than the Queens' mind games."

"Yeah, You're right," Leah said, straightening up and wincing from her sore muscles. "But maybe we can do this in the morning? I'm exhausted."

Sarah nodded. "Good call. I could use a little shuteye."

As they settled back into their beds, Leah couldn't stop thinking of all the unanswered questions. The static, the essence, the attack. It had to be connected. More importantly, was this a sign they weren't safe, and that Legion could be on them at any minute?

As the light flickered out, Leah closed her eyes, willing sleep to come.

"I need to talk to you about what happened in the alley," Asmodeus's voice echoed in the darkness.

Leah sat at the round marble table in their shared mental space, elbows resting on its cold surface as she fidgeted. Asmodeus paced the room, his starry eyes fixed on the floor, lost in thought.

"Glad to see you aren't burnt to a crisp." Leah shook her head. "What do you want?"

"The fire I grabbed. I don't know what it is exactly," he muttered. "It felt like a new well that called us, but different."

Leah recalled the sensation of being in two places at

once, something she'd nearly forgotten as she was being beaten. "It was like there were two of me."

Asmodeus continued his restless movement, ignoring her. Leah waited, tension building in her shoulders.

Finally, he spoke. "The two flames called to me in whispers, almost like *Nehemoth*, but there was chaos in the fire, like *Golohab*."

He paused, his back to Leah as he continued, "But we've used both before without the torches appearing. This was different."

Leah rubbed her temples, frustration seeping into her voice. "Torches? Care to elaborate?"

"When I help you with the Tree of Death, the wells come differently. This one felt like a choice," Asmodeus said. "One I had to make then, or not at all."

"That's strange." Leah frowned. "What happened when the flames took you?"

Asmodeus turned to face her, his starry eyes unreadable. "I heard a faint echo, a voice saying *Satariel*. After that, I split, same as you."

Leah leaned back in her chair. "I heard that too. *Satariel...* I could ask Isaac to see if he has heard it before. We need to be careful though. We don't know what effects it will have on us."

Asmodeus approached the table, conjuring a small mug of green tea. "I know. Like I said, it was a decision I had to make. I suspect with the threat of your life, the Trees had options to protect you if we were willing to take them." He took a sip, his gaze distant. "There are no traces of corruption that I sense now, but I think it is wise we both rest. I'll do what I can to not access that energy again until we learn more."

Leah nodded as relief and unease settled in her chest.

As their shared mental space faded, she found herself back in the darkness of the tent, the soft breathing of Sarah and Isaac filling the air.

She stared at the canvas ceiling for a long while, her mind a whirlwind of questions.

CHAPTER 5
A TENSE MEETING

The cafeteria's fluorescent lights buzzed overhead as cold morning air seeped through the warehouse's metal walls. Leah pushed her oatmeal around the bowl, each movement sending dull throbs through her bruised ribs. Across the battered plastic table, Sarah and Isaac watched her.

"They really did a number on you, didn't they?" Sarah asked, eyes fixed on the bruise darkening Leah's cheek.

"Yeah," Leah touched the tender spot. "Note to self: avoid the brass knuckles if you can."

"Wait, what?" Sarah shouted. Several heads turned their way. She lowered her voice to a harsh whisper. "If I catch those assholes, they better pray they get a hit on me first."

Leah opened her mouth, but a familiar voice called out from behind her before she could respond.

"Good morning, Leah."

Nick's voice made her skin prickle. She turned to find Nick approaching, his pristine white Rook's cloak billowing in his wake.

"Nick," Leah managed a polite nod. "What brings you here?"

His eyes lingered on her bruised cheek. "Queen Helen sent me to fetch you. She wants to discuss some urgent matters."

Leah's stomach clenched. She hadn't spoken to Helen since the attack on headquarters, since watching Gabe die. Since everything fell apart.

"She hasn't spoken to me for weeks," Leah said. "What's changed?"

"I suppose she'll have to tell you that," Nick said. "She's asked for you now, so if you'll come with me."

"I'll catch up with you guys later," she told Sarah and Isaac, pushing herself up from the table.

The walk through camp was silent except for their boots crunching frozen ground. Mystics stopped to stare as they passed, whispering behind raised hands. The familiar weight of unwanted attention pressed down on her shoulders.

"So," Nick cleared his throat. "How are you holding up?"

"Fine," Leah said curtly, then sighed. "Sorry. It's just... a lot."

"I can't imagine what you're going through," Nick said, a touch of sympathy in his voice. "But if you ever need someone to talk to..."

"Thanks." Leah managed a small smile.

They approached a weathered Victorian house on the outskirts of the camp. Two Bishops stood guard at the door, faces impassive as Nick led her inside.

She followed him down a hallway, the floorboards creaking beneath their feet as they reached a closed door.

Nick knocked a quick succession of raps and waited.

"Come in," Helen called.

The office was small, with peeling wallpaper and a

musty smell that made Leah's nose wrinkle. Helen sat behind a cluttered desk, her skin sallow in the dim light. Dark circles shadowed her eyes, and her once-vibrant red hair was now full of gray streaks.

"Leah." Helen gestured to the chair in front of her. "Please, sit."

As Leah settled into the chair, she couldn't shake the feeling that something was off. The Helen before her wasn't the same woman who had fought beside her. This Helen seemed... hollow somehow.

"How have you been?" Helen asked, leaning forward slightly. "I know we haven't had much chance to talk since... everything."

Static buzzed faintly in Leah's ears. She saw Helen wince, one hand going to her neck.

Something's wrong with her energy, Asmodeus whispered. *It's corrupted*.

"I'm managing," Leah said carefully. "Trying to help where I can."

"Indeed, you have. You've become quite the inspiration, Leah. A true symbol of hope for our people."

The words caused Leah's chest to tighten. She shifted in her seat. "About that. I'm not sure I'm cut out for this 'war hero' role. I don't deserve it, not when other's have done so much more for the Board."

Helen's eyes hardened. "We all have our parts to play, Leah. Sometimes those parts are chosen for us." She paused, her tone shifting. "We have a new assignment for you. We're instituting joint training exercises between our younger members and the rootworkers. You'll be overseeing them."

"Is that safe? After everything that's happened?"

"There are always risks," Helen said. "But who better to keep our young members safe than you?"

Frustration built in Leah's chest. "With all due respect, shouldn't we be focusing on Legion? He's still out there, and we're sitting here playing politics."

Helen's nostrils flared. "Let us worry about Legion," she snapped.

"Let you worry about it?" Leah shot back. "Like you did at HQ? How many died because—"

Helen's fist slammed down on the desk. "Things are different now!"

The outburst hung between them. Helen took a deep breath, composing herself.

"We are in a very fragile state," she continued, her voice low and tense. "We have few places we can be safe. Legion is targeting us directly. We can't afford internal strife or questioning of authority. Not now."

The static in Leah's ears grew louder. She saw Helen touch her neck again, pain flickering across her face.

"I didn't mean—" Leah began, but Helen waved her off.

"I know," Helen sighed. "These are stressful times."

After a moment of silence, Leah asked, "Has there been any news? About Legion, since the attack?"

Helen hesitated. "He hasn't been spotted since you injured him. But his forces are still active. Coordinated attacks." Her eyes blazed suddenly with fierce intensity. "I'm hunting him down personally. Following every lead, every whisper."

"Should you be telling me this?"

"You deserve to know. Because despite our... differences, I trust you." Helen leaned back, looking exhausted. "And because I need you to understand why these joint exercises and maintaining our alliances are so crucial. We need every advantage when the time comes to face Legion again."

Leah nodded slowly, the weight of Helen's words settling over her.

"Will you lead the exercises?" Helen asked, her tone making it clear it wasn't really a question.

Leah looked down at her hands, Helen's words forming a knot in her stomach. She'd always guided her and protected her, too, but lately, every interaction felt more and more like a game she didn't get to know the rules to. Still, what choice did she have? "Yes. I'll do it."

"Good. Report to the front of the cafeteria this afternoon. You'll be escorted into town." As Leah stood to leave, Helen called out. "And Leah? Be careful. There are forces at work here beyond what you can see. Trust your instincts."

Leah paused at the door, looking back at the woman who had been her mentor, her guide, and now... something else entirely. "I will."

Outside in the gray morning, she leaned against the house's weathered siding, her mind spinning.

Well, Asmodeus mused, *that was certainly interesting.*

"Yeah," Leah whispered, touching her bruised ribs. "Interesting is one word for it."

CHAPTER 6
JOINT EXERCISES

The Squares' excited chatter echoed off the brick walls as Leah led them through Sekrè Fami. Sarah and Isaac flanked the group while their two escorts maintained a careful distance. Ashley's voice carried over the others as she pointed out all the graffiti to Zoe, who nodded silently, taking in everything. The energy built beneath Leah's skin, pressing against her still bruised ribs as she readied to react at the first sign of trouble as locals stared at them passing by.

She caught Jenna hanging back again, hands stuffed in her pockets. But her usual scowl had softened to curiosity as the smell of fresh bread wafted from a nearby bakery. Ricky walked near her, likely unaware that Jenna was using his bulk as a buffer between her and the suspicious looks from locals.

The escorts—a man and woman from Madeline's faction—kept scanning the streets, shoulders tense. Leah understood their wariness. Despite Helen's influence, getting Madeline to agree to these training sessions had taken days of negotiation. Bringing young Mystics into rootworker territory remained dangerous, regardless of any truce.

"Callum!" Her voice cracked like a whip as she saw the gangly boy stepping onto the road toward the bakery. His freckled face turned up toward the shop's sign. "Sidewalk! Now!"

The boy jumped back from the street, nearly colliding with Zoe. His cheeks flushed bright red beneath his freckles. "Sorry, Knight Ackerman!"

Leah shook her head, fighting a small smile. These kids lived in their own world, untouched by the darkness that haunted her dreams. Even Ricky, usually so skeptical, was distracted by the town's sights and sounds. She envied that, remembering when school had been her biggest worry.

Ashley looked back at the bakery as she piped up, "Can we get pastries on the way back?"

"We don't have money," Leah said. The girl's face fell, her usual enthusiasm dimming, and something twisted in Leah's chest. "But I'll ask next time if this goes well."

Excited whispers rippled through the group. Ashley grabbed Zoe's arm, already planning what they'd try first. Callum's gangly frame straightened while Ricky tried and failed to hide his own interest. Even Jenna perked up slightly at the prospect, though she quickly schooled her expression.

Isaac dropped back, falling in step beside her. His eyes glowed faintly yellow as he scanned the street. "You're getting better at this," he whispered. "I know a few Bishops who could take some pointers."

She shrugged. "Hard not to preserve that innocence, you know?"

Isaac nudged her shoulder. "You know you have us, right? You're not alone."

Leah absently rubbed her palm, remembering the strange power she'd accessed in that alley. "Actually... there is something I wanted to ask you about." She glanced around, making sure none of the Squares were within earshot. "Have you ever heard of something called *Satariel*?"

Isaac's eyes unfocused, as if he were filing through all the books and notes he'd read. "Can't say that I have. Why?"

Leah opened her mouth to explain but caught Jenna lingering a little too close. "Just... something I came across in some old texts," she said carefully. "Would you mind looking into it?"

"Of course." Isaac studied her face for a moment. "You know you can tell me anything, right?"

"I know." Leah managed a small smile. "Let's just focus on keeping these kids safe for now."

"Totally." His gaze settled on her. "And how's... everything else?"

Leah's jaw tightened. She knew what he was really asking—how was she coping?

"I'm fine." She sighed at his skeptical look, then rolled her eyes. "Okay, *not* fine. But I'm managing."

Isaac nudged her shoulder. "You know you have us, right? You're not alone."

They rounded a corner onto the main street. It looked vastly different from when she'd walked it with Jaime—no music or drunks dancing. Just ordinary people going about their day, though many stared at the group of young Mystics.

Energy hummed beneath Leah's skin as she straightened her shoulders. Hero or not, she wouldn't let them see her falter.

"We're here," their female escort announced, gesturing to a weathered building. Peeling paint revealed old brick underneath, and a sign above the door read "4th St Boxing."

Leah frowned but ushered her Squares inside, Isaac and Sarah flanking the group. She nodded to their escorts. "Thank you."

The two jerked their heads in acknowledgment, taking positions on either side of the glass door. Leah took a deep breath, reaching instinctively for her connection to the Tree of Life, and stepped inside.

A loud, booming chime pierced the air. By reflex, energy surged through Leah's veins as her hand flew to her side, heart hammering against her ribs. For a terrible moment, she was back at headquarters—explosions rocking the building, screams filling the air, the acrid smell of smoke...

Breathe. Focus, Asmodeus's voice cut through the memory. *We're not there anymore.*

"First time boxing?" a deep voice asked, pulling her back to the present.

Leah breathed in slowly and blinked. A broad-shouldered man in a black hoodie and gym logo for 4th Street Boxing watched her, his eyes knowing. Not pity, just understanding.

"Yeah," she managed. "You could say that."

He nodded, extending a hand. "Name's Mark. I'm training your... uh, Squares... today. My co-trainer Claire will be helping out as well." He gestured to a tall woman with curly hair and an orange shirt bearing the same logo.

Leah shook his hand. "Leah Ackerman. Black Knight of the Infinity Board."

Recognition flickered in Mark's eyes, but he didn't comment on her title. "Pleasure to meet you. Your group can grab some jump ropes and start warming up with the others."

She watched her Squares join about fifteen local

teenagers already skipping rope. The Tree's energy hummed through the room as the two groups sized each other up. Some of the town's kids eyed the newcomers warily, whispering. One boy snorted with laughter when he spotted Jenna, though he quickly looked away when Leah's gaze found him.

Gathering her Squares close, she leaned in. "Listen up. I know this is new, but we're Mystics. We've trained hard, too. Play by their rules, but know you can beat them." Her voice hardened. "But no Tree here. This is physical only. Got it?"

Ashley bounced on her toes while Callum cracked his knuckles and looked nervously around. Zoe gave a small nod, already studying the boxing equipment with careful consideration. Only Ricky crossed his arms, surveying the room slowly.

"What if they try something first?" he asked.

"Then you prove you're better than that," Leah said, catching Jenna's eye where she hung at the back of the group. The girl's thin frame was tense, but Leah saw a glimmer of interest breaking through her usual indifference.

As her group dispersed to grab equipment, Leah swept the gym. Boxing bags hung from metal trusses, and a ring dominated the far corner next to a lifting station. She approached it, running her fingers along the canvas. Memories of countless matches in the Academy's octagon flooded back.

A strange tingling sensation prickled her fingertips, different from the Tree's familiar energy. Leah frowned, bringing her hand closer to examine it. The feeling vanished as quickly as it had come.

"Weird," she muttered.

Something's off about this place, Asmodeus observed.

Mark's voice boomed over the speakers. "Crew, partner up with one of these Mystics. I don't want to see a single one of them without a partner, you hear? Help them get their hands wrapped, too."

Leah turned, relieved to see all her Squares, even Jenna, pairing up without issue. As Mark moved among the students, checking hand-wraps, the gym's door opened.

A bald man with copper skin entered, fist-bumping Mark and handing him a manila folder. Recognition jolted through her. Although he was more solid than the last time she saw him; he was the same essence that eavesdropped on the Queens' meeting. The newcomer's dark eyes scanned the room, landing on Leah. His expression shifted, and he turned abruptly, heading for the exit.

Energy surged through Leah's veins. Without thinking, she moved to follow.

"Keep an eye on the Squares," she called to Sarah.

Isaac caught her arm as she passed. "Where are you going?"

"I'll be right back!"

She burst onto the street, glimpsing the man ducking into a narrow alley. Leah sprinted after him, her footsteps echoing off brick walls covered in graffiti. We Remember 1891, the message repeated over and over.

Her target was fast, but Leah was driven by more than physical speed. She gathered her energy for a *Malchut* push, feeling it build like lightning in her chest. Time slowed as she launched forward, her shoulder connecting with the man's back.

They tumbled together, rough concrete scraping Leah's palms as she pinned him down. Power thrummed through her arms as she gripped his shirt. "Who are you?"

"Careful," he said, raising his hands in surrender. His

thick French accent took her by surprise. "You're ruining the shirt."

"I asked you a question," Leah growled.

"Claude," he said, his voice cold. "And you are?"

"Leah Ackerman."

Claude's eyes narrowed slightly. "You Jewish?"

Heat billowed up her neck. "Yeah. Got a problem with that?"

"Just like your kind to stick your nose where it doesn't belong," he spat. "Always thinking you can walk into places you don't belong."

Leah's grip tightened on his shirt. Through gritted teeth, she said, "Why were you spying on us?"

Claude looked left and right, seeing onlookers at both ends of the alley. A sneer spread across his face. "Better release me before you make more enemies than you can handle, little girl."

She followed his gaze and saw the growing crowd. Reluctantly, she pushed off him, but kept her hands balled into fists as she backed away.

"Nothing to see here," Claude called out to the crowd as he stood, brushing dirt from his clothes. "Just another Mystic where they don't belong."

Leah glared at him, but the alley cleared as the bystanders went about their business. She turned to him, ready to pounce.

"Why were you spying on us?"

He crossed his arms. "Us? I recall you were spying, too."

Leah smiled as she held up the small voodoo doll necklace she'd torn from his neck during their tumble. With that, Claude's cocky demeanor faltered.

"One *Malchut* push, and you're dead," Leah said, laying a finger on his chest. "So, start talking."

Claude regained his composure. "One *Malchut* push and your truce with the Sekrè Fami is over."

"Killing a rootworker who was spying on our leadership?" Leah countered. "I'll take my chances."

They locked eyes, neither willing to back down. Claude seemed to weigh his options. Finally, he smiled and raised his hands in mock surrender.

"Fair enough," he said. "I'm one of the 1891. We don't trust you or Madeline, so we do what we need to keep our people safe."

"We're not here to fight you," Leah insisted. "We're here to regroup and fight Legion."

Claude's eyes hardened. "So, you say. Given our history with Mystics, you can't blame us for being cautious. Even if some are eager to help."

"Madeline trusted the Infinity Board because Nykima fought Legion with us. She's in a wheelchair because of that monster."

"That's *your* truth," Claude shot back. "To us, we see a grandmother being swayed by a traitor who deserted us long ago and came back because she was cornered. There's a reason Sekrè Fami has survived this long. We've kept to ourselves. There's no need to change that now."

Leah stepped closer, her nose inches from Claude's. "Legion is your problem, too, whether you like it or not."

Claude shrugged. "I haven't heard of him attacking any other voodoo towns. Why should we risk our people for you?"

"Because he'll come for you next!"

"We've been fine without your 'protection.'" Claude mimicked air quotes. "Besides, there's a reason you're all hiding here."

Leah backed away, letting out a huff. How could someone be so stubborn? So blind to the bigger threat?

"Well, this was nice, but I'll be on my way," Claude said, turning to leave. Leah's hand shot out, gripping his arm.

"Did you do that spell on me? Send in your cronies to attack me?"

Claude frowned. "The guys who jumped you did it because you were an intruder in our district. No one comes in unnoticed. Better remember that for next time."

He tried to pull away, but Leah held firm. "What about that spell? The static that stunned me while I was chasing you?"

"Spell?" Claude scoffed. "I don't know what you're talking about." He yanked his arm free. "Are we done here, or are you looking for another fight?"

Leah studied him for a moment. Then, she held out the necklace. "Here. Wouldn't want you to forget this."

Claude hesitated, then took the necklace, turned and walked away, as he placed the necklace around his neck.

She watched the man disappear around a corner, energy still pressed against her skin. If that static wasn't them, then who did it?

Well, that was certainly interesting, Asmodeus mused as Leah jogged back toward the gym.

"Not now," Leah muttered.

Oh, come now, the demon pressed. *You can't tell me you're not curious about what's really going on. That static wasn't normal.*

As much as she hated to admit it, he had a point. There were too many unanswered questions. And if she wasn't careful, the Squares she aimed to protect would be caught in the middle.

She quickened her pace. She'd play along with this "joint training" charade for now. But she'd be damned if she let her guard down again.

CHAPTER 7

A FAVOR

Sweat trickled down Leah's neck as she slipped back into the gym, the smell of leather and chalk thick in the air. Sarah caught her eye, questions written across her face, but maintained her position watching the Squares. At least someone was following protocol.

Your little chase accomplished nothing, Asmodeus drawled in her mind, *except maybe aggravating those injuries.*

"Not now," Leah muttered under her breath, scanning the room. Her Squares were scattered throughout the space, each showing off the results of her months of training them. Ricky gave his punches natural weight but telegraphed his movements too much. Callum's gangly limbs actually worked to his advantage, giving him unexpected reach that surprised his sparring partner. Zoe, a bit on the smaller side, focused on perfecting each movement just as she did with her *Malchut* training, allowing her sparring partner to show her a few new moves.

To her surprise, they seemed to get along with the local kids, sharing tips on stance and form. Even Jenna lost some of her usual scowls as she worked with a girl about her size, showing the same careful control she had brought to practice.

"Knight Ackerman! Watch this!" Ashley called out, hopping up and down. She demonstrated a combination they'd practiced last week. "Did you see that? Just like you showed us—jab, cross, weave!"

Ashley had always been a quick study, the first to volunteer for demonstrations. Her eagerness sometimes got ahead of her technique, but her athleticism made up for it.

Leah managed a smile. "Nice work. Keep it up." The words felt hollow in her mouth, but at least Ashley smiled back before turning back to her punching bag, already starting another combination.

Leah's mind reeled as she led the Squares back to camp, her senses on high alert. The streets felt too exposed, with too many shadows for enemies to lurk.

The makeshift cafeteria's fluorescent lights buzzed overhead as her Squares rushed for food, their earlier exertion fueling ravenous appetites. Leah hung back with Sarah and Isaac, waiting for the initial rush to die down.

"So," Sarah said, her voice low and eager, "are you going to tell us why you bolted from the gym?"

Leah noticed a group of Knights passing their table, huddled together. She caught fragments of their conversation about shifter movements near the Canadian border. Her stomach clenched. Their expansion north meant Legion's influence was spreading. She leaned in close to her friends, keeping her voice barely above a whisper. "I found our spy. The one from the Queens' meeting."

Sarah's eyes widened while Isaac's brow furrowed in that familiar way when his mind kicked into overdrive.

"What happened?" Sarah pressed, her words tumbling out in a rush.

Leah recounted her encounter with Claude.

"So, they're actively spying on us," Isaac mused, absently touching the dark scar on his face. "But why? What do they want?"

"Leverage," Sarah said, stabbing her mashed potatoes with enough force to make the tray rattle. "If they know what we know, then we can't surprise them."

Same as you, Asmodeus chimed in. *It's not like your Queens have been exactly forthcoming with their plans.*

Leah pushed away the demon's words along with her untouched food. "It's just... frustrating. We're in the middle of a war with Legion, and we're stuck playing petty politics with the locals."

"Petty politics indeed," a familiar monotone voice cut in.

They turned to find Eli standing beside their table, holding a tray of food with white gloves that matched his pristine white Rook's cloak. His tired eyes carried that same unnerving intensity she remembered from headquarters.

"Care if I join?" he asked, his expression unreadable.

The trio exchanged a look before Sarah shrugged. "Sure, why not?"

Eli set his tray beside Sarah, a neatly arranged turkey sandwich and a small pile of potato chips. He took a bite, chewing slowly as the others stared.

After a moment of awkward silence, Eli looked up. "What?"

"You don't usually eat with us," Leah said. "Or really with anyone."

"Is there a problem?" Eli asked.

"No," Leah said. "I mean, I'm just... curious about the reason."

Eli sighed, setting down his sandwich. "If you must know, I need to ask you something."

Sarah leaned forward, a mischievous glint in her eye. "Oh, really? I couldn't tell. So, what does the great *Bonded* need from us?"

Eli's expression remained unreadable, but Leah caught the faintest blush on his cheeks. He cleared his throat, fidgeting with his napkin. "As you know, the Queens are interested in promoting more mingling with the rootworkers. Tonight, they're organizing a social gathering with Madeline to, as they put it, 'promote tolerance and boost morale.'"

Leah watched Eli's fingers twist the napkin into knots, a rare show of nerves from the usually composed Rook. Something about this request clearly made him uncomfortable, and that piqued her interest.

"And what? You're inviting us?" Leah prompted.

Eli sighed, his shoulders slumping slightly. "Look, social events are... not my thing. Actually, they're the worst. But the Queens need people to attend. People with status...." He trailed off, looking anywhere but at them.

Sarah leaned forward. "Wait, are you asking us to go in your place?"

"Yes. That would be correct," Eli said.

Isaac frowned. "But why us? Surely there are other Rooks or Bishops who could attend."

"You three have proven yourselves capable. Leah, you're our... war hero," Eli said with a look of distaste. "And you two helped save the Sages. You'll fit in far better than I would."

The familiar weight of expectations pressed down on

Leah's shoulders. She opened her mouth to protest, but Sarah beat her to it.

"Hold up," Sarah said. "So, we get to go to a fancy Mystic party after months of living like...this?"

"It's not a party," Eli corrected. "It's a diplomatic function. And yes, that's what I'm proposing."

Isaac shifted in his seat. "But won't they wonder where you are?"

Eli waved a dismissive hand. "Just say I was indisposed, and you're there on my behalf."

Leah weighed her options, recognizing she couldn't get away from being touted as a hero if she were to go, noting how an event like this could help them. Or at least get her a chance to see what the Queens were up to.

"And you're certain they won't kick us out when we show up?" Leah asked.

Eli shrugged. "Maybe, but Helen wanted you there. It was Micah and Jan who said no. But if you show up, how could they turn you away?"

Sarah grinned. "You sure have tricks for someone who doesn't like playing the Board's games."

"Have to know the game to avoid it," Eli said, standing and picking up his tray. "Be at Le Syndicat at eight. Formal uniforms. And try to blend in."

As Eli turned to leave, the weight of her earlier discovery pressed her. She couldn't let him walk away without warning him. "Wait," she called out. "I need to tell you something."

Eli paused. "Yes?"

Leah took a deep breath. "You and the Queens are being spied on. I saw a rootworker during your meeting last night. I... I snuck in using *Thagirion* to eavesdrop. That's how I spotted him."

She braced herself for Eli's anger, but to her surprise, he

was unfazed. "I know. I sensed you both as soon as I entered the house."

Leah's jaw dropped. "You did? But... why did you let us stay?"

Eli shifted his weight as if he were contemplating his words. "We know they are spying. If we were discussing truly sensitive information, neither of you would have heard it."

"So, you aren't concerned?" Leah pressed, her voice rising.

Eli's expression softened. "The 1891 faction doesn't trust us. We spy on them, and they spy on us. The information they report back is controlled, and it only furthers the need for an alliance between them, the Infinity Board, and Madeline."

Heat crept up Leah's neck. She'd thought she was being so clever when she spied, but she fell right into their trap.

"Why did you let me stay?" she asked.

Eli's gaze met hers, and momentarily, she saw a slight smile. "Helen is fond of you three. And to be honest, so am I. I took a calculated risk to help hasten to bring you into the fold."

"Wait," Isaac blurted out. "Are you saying what I think you're saying?"

Eli smiled at Isaac. "Always the brains of the group. But please, excuse me, I have work to do. Good luck tonight."

As Eli walked away, Leah rounded on Isaac. "What? What did he mean?"

Isaac smirked and shook his head. "He knew you'd follow. Probably figured you'd end up in a fight, too."

"That asshole," Sarah said.

Leah pushed herself up from the table, grinning. "Asshole, maybe, but at least he's on our side."

“And now we have a party to go to,” Sarah said,
following Leah.

CHAPTER 8

LE SYNDICAT

The vanilla-scented air washed over Leah as she pushed through the heavy door of Le Syndicat, Sarah and Isaac following close behind. Her fitted black blazer and slacks, borrowed from the Knight's supply closet, matched the formal attire she'd seen others wear as they approached. The familiar bar brought back memories of her last visit with Alma, though everything felt different now.

Sarah had convinced one of the Bishops to loan her a burgundy dress shirt with her white uniform pants. Beside her, Isaac kept it simple in his Bishop's formal wear—pressed black slacks and a crisp white button-down.

Through the dim lighting, she caught the bouncer's skeptical stare. He was the same dark-skinned man with intricate tattoos snaking up his muscular arms. His eyes narrowed as they approached.

"IDs," he grunted, his deep voice rumbling.

Sarah cleared her throat, squaring her shoulders. "We're here on behalf of Eli Abrams, White Rook and Sage of the Infinity Board."

The bouncer's expression remained impassive, unimpressed by the name-drop. "This is a private event. No underage entrance. Get out of here."

Sarah glanced back at Leah and Isaac, uncertainty flickering across her face.

Not ready to give up that easily, Leah stepped forward, meeting the bouncer's gaze. "We're just looking for something sweet, with a hint of vanilla," she said. "Promise we won't cause any trouble."

The bouncer's eyebrow arched slightly, a flicker of recognition passing over him as he looked at Leah. After a moment's hesitation, he reached for the door handle.

"What's in the bag?" he asked abruptly, his eyes fixed on the small black backpack slung over Leah's shoulder.

"I told you to leave it at home," Sarah hissed.

Leah slipped the bag off her shoulder, unzipping it to reveal its contents. "It's just a book." The tome containing Tom's spirit felt heavier than usual under the bouncer's scrutiny.

He peered inside. After what felt like an eternity, he stepped back, pulling the door open without another word.

As they stepped into the bar proper, Sarah turned to Leah with wide eyes. "How'd you know how to get us in?"

Leah tapped her nose. "The vanilla smell is like a code word if you're here on business. Learned that when I was with Alma."

"Nice," Isaac said. He scanned the crowded space. "Now what?"

Sarah's arms snaked around their shoulders, pulling them close. "What else would we do in a bar? We drink!" she declared with infectious enthusiasm as she steered them through the throng of bodies.

The bar was a far cry from Leah's last visit. Mystics in their distinctive uniforms mingled with elegantly dressed rootworkers, their laughter and chatter blending with the sultry jazz floating through the air. Near the center of the room, Leah spotted Queen Helen, Queen Micah, and Madeline, surrounded by a cluster of White Knights and Bishops, deep in conversation.

Leah shivered as a familiar presence materialized beside her. "I don't detect any dormant demons," Tom's ghostly voice whispered.

"You good?" Isaac asked Leah.

Leah nodded. "Yeah, I'm fine." She turned slightly, addressing the spectral boy. "Thanks, Tom. Just... maybe give me a heads up before appearing right next to me next time?"

A smooth jazz cut through the crowd, drawing Leah toward a small stage tucked into the corner. The pianist—a large Black man with broad shoulders—sat hunched over the keys, lost in his own world as his fingers danced along the keys. His tailored suit caught the stage lights, making him look almost ethereal as a quartet behind him wove their instruments around his lead.

"I'm telling you, this woman does not waste a second," Isaac's exasperated voice cut through her reverie. Leah followed his eyes to find Sarah at the bar, already deep in conversation with a gorgeous bartender in a low-cut dress.

Leah chuckled. "I'm glad. Especially after Yuki ghosted her."

"Sure," Isaac grumbled, nodding to the growing line of patrons waiting behind her. "But there are other people who want to order."

Leah waved a dismissive hand. "Ah, let her have some fun. There are other bartenders they can go to." She nudged Isaac's shoulder. "You know you could try to meet someone. Plenty of hot people around."

Isaac paled as he ran a hand through his short hair. "Uh, sure, maybe."

Leah's brow furrowed, sensing there was more to his hesitation. "Seems like you might have someone in—"

"Got us free drinks!" Sarah said as she materialized between them with three tall glasses balanced precariously in her hands.

"Nice!" Isaac said, accepting a glass. "What are they?"

Sarah shrugged and laughed. "No idea. I just asked her to make us something good."

Leah eyed the drink. "That's like the worst thing you can do unless you want to black out."

"Oh, stop whining and have some!" Sarah insisted, pressing a glass into Leah's hand.

The liquid was bitter with an underlying sweetness, leaving a faint burn in her throat. Isaac coughed as he took a sip, which made both Sarah and Leah laugh.

"Woah, slow down there," Leah said.

They drifted closer to the band, letting the jazz wash over them

Such control and precision, Asmodeus mused. *It's almost... magical.*

Leah suppressed a smile at the demon's uncharacteristic fascination. "What do you think of it?"

It's... soothing, he admitted after a moment. *I can see why humans find it so captivating.*

As the song ended, Sarah lifted her empty glass and signaled to Leah she was heading for more. Isaac opened his mouth to protest, but Leah elbowed him. "You know it's just an excuse to let her talk to the bartender, right?"

Isaac paused, then nodded. "Oh... yeah. Obviously."

Leah noticed his gaze drift towards the entrance, the color draining from his face. She followed his line of sight, spotting Mark and Claire from the boxing gym as they entered the bar. Isaac swallowed hard and smoothed down his hair.

A smirk tugged at Leah's lips. "Oh look, Mark and Claire are here."

"What? Oh, yeah," Isaac stammered. "I'm, uh... I'm gonna head to the restroom. I'll find you in a bit."

Before Leah could respond, Isaac disappeared into the crowd. She shook her head, taking another sip of her drink as she drifted through the sea of bodies. Without her friends as buffers, she became acutely aware of the stares directed her way. Mystics whispered behind raised hands, their eyes following her every move.

She took a longer gulp of her drink, wincing at the burn, and approached the bar. At least there, she could blend in with the crowd around Sarah.

"Leah! I didn't expect you to be here."

The familiar Scottish brogue cut through the din. Leah turned to find Rook Jaime McMillan, his cheeks flushed and a glass of scotch in hand. Flanking him were two Black Rooks—a slender woman with long, raven hair and a man with a neatly trimmed beard and piercing blue eyes.

Leah smiled. "Good to see you again, Rook McMillan."

Jaime gestured towards his companions. "I have a feeling you three have met before."

The bearded man's eyes lit with recognition. "We did. You took shifts at the bar and back at HQ, right? You're Elizabeth's daughter?"

Memories of nights at the headquarters bar flooded back, and Leah nodded. "Oh yeah, I remember seeing you at the bar." She racked her brain for their names but came up blank.

The woman extended a hand. "I'm Whitney, and this is my partner, Elliot."

Leah shook their hands, grateful that Whitney saved Leah from embarrassing herself.

Elliot's grip was firm, his eyes intense as he spoke. "May

I just say thank you for what you did at HQ? If it wasn't for you, I don't know if we would have made it out of that battle alive."

A familiar voice echoed in Leah's mind, laden with pain. *"Please! Go!"*

Gabe's last words hit her hard. The weight of all she'd lost, all she'd sacrificed, threatened to overwhelm her. She took in a slow breath.

"I was just doing my duty," Leah managed, her throat tight.

"Nonsense!" Elliot insisted. "Let us buy you a drink. They have this fantastic rum drink you have to try."

"I think Leah's looking for her friends," Jaime interjected.

Leah forced a smile as she turned her focus back to the conversation. "Yeah, sorry. I was just about to catch up with them." A lie.

"I see," Elliot said. "Well, next time, then."

"Come on, love," Whitney said, linking her arm with Elliot's. "We need to show these rootworkers that some Mystics can actually dance."

"Don't forget about me," Jaime said. He downed the rest of his drink. "I know a mean merengue."

Leah mouthed a silent "thank you" to Jaime as the trio made their way to the dance floor.

Leah scanned the room, searching for a familiar face among the sea of strangers. Her eyes landed on a small, empty table tucked away in a corner. A painting of a large Black man playing a trombone hung on the wall above, but it was the solitary figure seated beneath it that caught Leah's attention.

"Nykima," she breathed, recognizing the slumped shoulders and defeated posture of the former White Knight.

Leah weaved through the crowd, approaching the table with caution. Nykima sat hunched over her drink.

"I never took you for a loner," Leah said softly, sliding into the empty chair across from her.

Nykima's head snapped up, and she focused her blood-shot eyes on Leah. "O-oh, look wh-who it is," she slurred, her attention dropping to Leah's insignia. "Black Knight Ackerman. Or should I say, war hero?"

The acrid smell of vodka rolled off Nykima's breath, making Leah wince. "I... how are you?"

"I'm marvelous," Nykima declared, punctuating her statement with a large gulp of her drink.

Leah hesitated for a moment, then asked. "What happened? After the battle at HQ?"

"I was arrested," Nykima said, her words slightly garbled. "Then I..." Her voice trailed off, and she looked past Leah.

"Would you like water?" Leah suggested, reaching for Nykima's glass. "I could get you—"

The older woman's hand shot out with surprising speed, gripping Leah's wrist. "Don't touch my drink."

Leah withdrew her hand slowly. "Oh, I'm sorry. I didn't mean to...."

Nykima's shoulders sagged. The fight drained out of her. "I'm surprised you want to sit with me."

Leah frowned. "Why would you even say that?"

Nykima rested her head in her hand, gesturing broadly at the crowded bar with her drink. "Half of these bastards think I'm a spy for the rootworkers, and the other half think I'm a spy for the Mystics." She took another long swig. "So here I am, a spy for neither but hated by both."

Leah leaned in. "That's bullshit. If it weren't for you, more would have died. You're a White Kni—"

Nykima's fist slammed onto the table, the sharp crack

making Leah jump. "I'm nothing!" The raw pain in her voice cut through Leah like a knife. "My title's been stripped. I've been questioned, used, and traded back to the people I left." She raised her cup in a mocking toast. "You're the hero they want, Leah Ackerman."

The words hit Leah in the gut, the shame and guilt churning her insides. How was it possible that Nykima had been treated this way? While Leah had been treated like a hero, showered with praise she didn't deserve.

"I..." Leah began, but the words caught in her throat. What could she possibly say to make this right?

Before she could respond, someone else approached the table. Madeline stood beside their table, her brown eyes tinged with yellow as she regarded them both.

"Bonswa, Leah," the Voodoo Queen said. "It's been a long time." Her gaze flickered to Nykima, who seemed unphased by her grandmother's sudden appearance. "I'd like a word, please."

Leah blinked, surprised by the request. She pulled herself out of the booth and stood.

"I'm sorry for bothering you," Leah said.

Nykima finished her drink and slammed it down. "See you around, war hero."

CHAPTER 9
QUEENS

Leah's throat tightened as Nykima's bitter words echoed in her mind. Guilt pressed down on her shoulders, and each step toward Madeline felt heavier than the last. As she approached the Voodoo Queen, the cacophony of voices and clinking glasses faded into a dull roar.

Madeline stopped at the top of a set of dark stairs leading down into the cellar. As Leah drew closer, she breathed in the woman's earthy and floral perfume.

"Bonswa, Leah," Madeline said. "It's been quite some time."

Leah nodded, struggling to find her voice. "Yeah, it has."

Madeline reached into her pocket, and her eyes flickered a yellowish glow as she studied Leah. "You've changed, child. The weight of war has done a number on you."

Leah opened her mouth to respond but froze as a thunderous sound echoed from the stairwell. She peered into the dark, but she couldn't see anything. Footsteps sounded on the steps below, and she backed up.

"What is that?" she whispered.

Madeline looked down the stairwell and smiled. "Nothing of concern yet." Her gaze pierced into Leah. "Tell me, child. Do you still seek vengeance for your mother's death?"

The question caught Leah off guard. Memories she'd long since buried dredged up. Her mother's lifeless body intertwined with Asmodeus chasing after her. She swallowed hard. "I... I don't know anymore."

"Hmm." Madeline put her hand on her chin. "A year and a half ago, you came here seeking your mother's killer. Today, you stand here bonded to that killer." Her eyes narrowed. "Are you certain you can trust him?"

Something at the base of the steps let out a low and rumbling moan and took another step up the stairs.

Leah called on *Tiferet*, peering into the dark. But before she could see the thing, Madeline gripped Leah's chin with surprising strength and forced Leah to look at her.

"Drop your *Tiferet*," she commanded.

Leah's breath caught in her throat. For a moment, she considered resisting, but reluctantly, she let her connection to *Tiferet* fade.

Madeline's eyes continued to glow as she peered into Leah's eyes. The sounds from the bar faded away, leaving only the sound of Leah's heart pounding in her ears.

After what felt like an eternity, Madeline released her grip. Leah stumbled back. Her nostrils flared.

"What the hell was that about?"

"Forgive me," Madeline said, her eyes dimming. "I needed to be certain we could trust this demon inside you. They make things... complicated. Yet, with his help, you are doing things no one has seen in a long time. Abilities too corrupted for one person to wield." She leaned close and whispered, "Should you need anything, call on me, and I will come."

"Thanks." Leah bit her lip. "This 1891 faction. Are you worried they might try something?"

Madeline let out a chuckle. "Let them. It would give me an excuse to finish what was started long ago. But unfortunately, their leaders are smarter than that. For now."

"Do you think they'll ever join the fight against Legion?"

"I hope not."

Leah frowned. "What? Why?"

Madeline rested a hand on her hip and sighed. "If they join our fight, then Legion would have drawn blood on my people first." She paused, her eyes finding Leah's. "Tell me, do you believe we can defeat him?"

The question hung heavy in the air. Leah's mind raced, images of the battle at HQ flashing before her eyes. The screams of the dying, the acrid smell of smoke and blood, Gabe's last moments...

"I don't know," she admitted. "If we could track him down. Like that ritual you did before, with Asmodeus."

Madeline shook her head. "You were marked by him. We don't have anything to track Legion down. But his hiding is a good sign."

"How so?"

"An opponent who hides is an opponent who can be defeated," Madeline said. "His attempt on your headquarters backfired, and you wounded him."

Before Leah could respond, a man in a three-piece suit approached. He leaned in close, whispering something in Madeline's ear. Her expression remained impassive, but Leah caught a flicker of something in her eyes. Concern? Anticipation?

"I see," Madeline murmured. She turned back to Leah. "It seems I'm needed elsewhere. It was good to finally catch up. Remember, you know where to find me should you need me."

With that, Madeline left, moving back into the crowd with effortless grace. Leah watched her go, a knot forming in her stomach. She glanced back at the stairwell, but whatever had lurked there was gone.

The bar's sounds rushed back in, a cacophony of laughter, clinking glasses, and snippets of conversation. Leah scanned the room, searching for Sarah and Isaac, and pressed into the crowd.

She could feel people's gazes turn to her as they recognized her.

"That's Leah Ackerman..."

"Elizabeth's daughter..."

"Who would have thought it'd run in the family?"

The whispers grew louder, and people pressed in on her from all sides. Leah's face burned, and her palms became slick with sweat. She wiped her palms on her pants, trying to steady her breathing.

The room spun, faces blurring together. Leah stumbled, bumping into a rootworker in a pristine white suit. She mumbled an apology, pushing past him.

That's when she saw him.

Tall, with that familiar shock of ashy hair. Leaning against the wall, his posture so achingly familiar it made her heart hurt.

"Gabe," Leah whispered.

She pushed through the crowd. It couldn't be him. No. But it looked just like him. "Gabe!" she called out, louder this time.

But as she drew closer, the man who looked like Gabe turned, and his features changed. It wasn't him. And the brief flicker of hope extinguished, leaving behind a void.

Leah's chest constricted, each breath straining against

her chest. The room tilted and swayed, faces blurring into a kaleidoscope of color and noise. She squeezed her eyes shut, but the images came anyway.

Explosions rocking the foundations of HQ. The agonized screams of her fellow Mystics. Gabe, his voice cracking with pain.

"Please! Go!"

Leah's eyes snapped open, but the memories refused to fade. With each blink, another horrific image assaulted her senses. Bodies of dead Mystics strewn across blood-soaked floors. The memory of Gabe pushing the remains of the mandrake potion into her chest.

"You have to." He looked up at the trees. "He'll help others. Save more people."

Leah's hand flew to her chest, phantom pain blossoming where the potion had seared her flesh. She could still feel Gabe's shaky fingers as she clung to him, refusing to let go.

The world narrowed to a pinpoint, and sounds became muffled and distorted. Leah's legs gave out, and she found herself on her knees, gasping for air that refused to come.

Leah, let me help you. Asmodeus's voice cut through the fog of panic as a man approached, his voice muffled and distorted.

Leah nodded. Or thought she did. The world tilted again, and then—

Darkness.

When Leah opened her eyes, she stood outside the bar, cold night air filling her lungs. She was seated on a low stone wall, her back pressed against rough brick. The muffled sounds of the party inside seemed a world away.

"What... what happened?" she mumbled, her throat raw.

You had a panic attack, Asmodeus explained. *I borrowed control for a moment to get us out here.*

Leah nodded, drawing in a shaky breath, then another, feeling her heartbeat slowly return to normal.

"Leah?"

She looked up and found Helen approaching, concern across her face as she crouched beside Leah. "Are you alright? I saw you rush out."

Leah opened her mouth to respond, but the words caught in her throat.

Helen's expression softened, and she nodded. "It's okay. You don't have to explain."

They sat in silence for a long moment, the distant sounds of the party echoing in the alley.

Finally, Leah asked, "How do you do it? How do you keep going, knowing what we've lost?"

Helen looked away, taking a deep breath before saying, "You just do. Because what else is there to do? Give up?"

"But is it all worth it?" Leah asked.

Helen rested a hand on Leah's knee. "It has to be. Because if it's not, it would all be for nothing."

Leah looked up at the night sky, following a cloud as it covered the crescent moon. "I don't know if I can do this," she admitted, her voice cracking. "Be this... symbol everyone needs me to be."

Helen squeezed Leah's knee. "You can. You're stronger than you realize. And we need the others to see that strength."

"But what if you're wrong and I'm not strong enough? What if I fail?"

"You have survived where others would have fallen. Time and time again, you've faced evil and pushed it away. You've accessed wells few can even comprehend. If that isn't strength, I don't know what is."

Leah wanted to believe her, but something gripped her chest and pulled her back.

Helen stood, gently pulling Leah to her feet. "Come on," she said, her voice taking on a lighter tone. "We should go back inside. I'll bet your friends are looking for you."

Leah nodded. "Yeah."

Just before they reached the door, Helen paused and said, "Remember that whatever comes, whatever sacrifices we must make, it's all for a greater purpose."

Leah met Helen's gaze, seeing the passion burning behind her eyes. She nodded, squaring her shoulders. She may not be strong, but she could pretend for Helen.

"I understand," Leah said.

And in that moment, she almost believed it.

CHAPTER 10
STATIC

The jazz from Le Syndicat still echoed in Leah's mind as she drifted into the darkness. Each note pulled her deeper into that dark, relieving her of her stress and tension until she found herself in a familiar space.

Asmodeus sat at a gleaming black piano, his pale fingers moving across the keys with a grace and ease as they mimicked the tunes played at Le Syndicat. The sight stopped Leah short.

She noted the shift in Asmodeus's form. His back was up straight and his face was soft. It was as if the music let him shed the remnants of his demonic form, if only for a moment.

The last notes faded, and Asmodeus's hands hovered over the keys, his starry eyes distant.

"I didn't know you could play," Leah whispered.

Asmodeus turned with a smirk on his face. "There's a lot you don't know about me."

Leah turned away, peering out into the dark. "It was beautiful."

He played a few more notes, then said, "I can see why humans find it so captivating."

Leah approached the piano, studying the demon's profile. "Is that why you brought me here? To show off your talents?"

Asmodeus chuckled. "As entertaining as that would be, we have more pressing matters to discuss." He stood, the piano vanishing as he did. The familiar round table materialized between them, two steaming mugs of tea waiting.

Leah sank into a chair, wrapping her hands around the warm mug. "Have you found anything else about the cloning trick we did?"

Asmodeus shook his head as he took the seat across from her. "No, but we need to understand it better. To control it."

"And how should we do that?" Leah arched an eyebrow. "We don't have much free time to practice potentially deadly magic."

"We would if we worked with the rootworkers," Asmodeus suggested. "Under supervision, of course."

Leah's stomach churned at the thought. After everything that had happened with the 1891 faction and her Squares, the idea of willingly putting herself in their hands seemed insane. "Are you serious?" she asked. "You really think we can trust them with this? If something goes wrong, and I lose control, all hell could break loose."

Asmodeus took a sip from his tea, then asked. "And how else do you expect us to grow stronger? To defeat Legion?" He leaned forward, his voice dropping to a low growl. "Or are you content to keep playing nursemaid to those Squares while the real threats gather at our doorstep?"

Leah pushed back from the table, standing so abruptly that her chair toppled. "That's not fair. You know why I'm training them. Someone has to make sure they're ready for what's coming."

"And who's making sure *you're* ready?" Asmodeus countered. "Have you looked around lately, Leah? Have you noticed how few older Mystics there are? There's a reason for that."

Memories of fallen Mystics flashing through Leah's her mind. She turned away, unable to face the truth in Asmodeus's words. "I can't be reckless with this power. Not when so many are counting on me."

Asmodeus moved behind her. "We don't have the luxury of caution anymore," he said. "You've seen what Legion is capable of. If we don't push ourselves or take risks, we won't stand a chance."

Leah closed her eyes, exhaling slowly. When she opened them, she stared at her reflection in a floor-length mirror that hadn't been there before. The girl who stared back looked older, wearier than she remembered. Expectations weighed her down.

"I'm scared," she whispered, the admission feeling like defeat and a release. "What if we go too far? What if we lose ourselves?"

Asmodeus's reflection appeared beside hers, his starry eyes meeting hers in the mirror. "We won't know unless we try. But doing nothing isn't an option anymore."

Leah nodded, a fragile resolve taking root in her chest. "Okay," she said. "We'll practice. Safely. And on my terms."

A hint of a smile crossed Asmodeus's lips. "I wouldn't expect anything less."

The mirror shimmered and faded, leaving them in the void of their shared consciousness. Leah turned to face Asmodeus directly.

"There's something else," she said. "At the bar, when

Madeline took me aside... there was something in the basement. Something that felt... wrong."

Asmodeus frowned. "Describe it."

Leah closed her eyes, recalling the thing she'd sensed. "It was big. Powerful. I could feel something else. It felt... hungry." She shuddered at the memory. "Madeline was controlling it, but barely."

"Interesting," Asmodeus mused. "Perhaps she's captured something with one of those many powders they make."

"Maybe," Leah said, unconvinced. "But this felt different. Wrong."

Before Asmodeus could respond, a piercing static cut into Leah's mind. She clutched her head, falling to the floor as the noise intensified. Through the buzz of static, she caught fragments of a voice.

"...help...Frank..."

"Leah!" Asmodeus's voice was distant, muffled by the static. "Focus on my voice. Come back to me."

The world spun, colors bleeding together as Leah pulled back to consciousness. She gasped, eyes flying open inside her tent, the faint glow of dawn seeping through the canvas walls.

The static continued, softer now but still present. Leah traced it back to Isaac's walkie-talkie, its display flickering with an eerie yellow light. She stumbled out of bed, ignoring her tired muscles as she grabbed the device.

"...please...anyone..." The voice was clearer now. "...Frank, where are you?"

Leah's fingers fumbled with the dials, trying to clear up the signal. "Hello?" she called into the receiver. "Who is this? Where are you?"

But the voice faded, replaced by a low hum that sent goosebumps down Leah's arm. The walkie-talkie grew hot in her hands, and she dropped it with a yelp as sparks erupted from its casing.

The tent flap burst open, Sarah stumbling in with Isaac close behind. "Are you okay?" Sarah asked, her words slightly slurred. "We heard shouting."

Leah stared at the smoking remains of the walkie-talkie, her heart pounding. "I... I don't know," she managed. "There was a voice. Someone calling for help."

Isaac frowned, kneeling to examine the device. "That's impossible. This thing's been dead for days."

"Well, it sure as hell wasn't dead a minute ago," Leah snapped, immediately regretting her tone as Isaac flinched. She took a deep breath, trying to calm her racing thoughts. "I'm sorry. It's just... it was the static I've been hearing. And there was this voice..."

Sarah frowned and looked at Isaac. "Leah, maybe you should sit down. You look like you're about to pass out."

"I'm fine," Leah said, right as her knees gave out and she stumbled toward the ground.

Isaac and Sarah caught her, easing her back into her cot.

"Deep breaths," Sarah said. "In through your nose, out through your mouth."

Leah tried to follow the instructions, but her lungs wouldn't expand. The edges of her vision darkened, and panic clawed at her throat. "I can't," she gasped. "I can't breathe."

Let me help, Asmodeus's voice cut through the fog of fear. *Trust me.*

Leah nodded, or thought she did. She felt a shift, like stepping back from herself, and suddenly, she was taking deep breaths again. She watched, as if from a great distance, as her body relaxed, her breathing evening out.

"That's it," Sarah murmured.

Control slowly returned to her, and she became aware of Isaac hovering nearby. "Should I get Helen?" he asked.

"No," Leah said quickly, her voice hoarse. "No, I'm... I'm alright." She managed a weak smile. "Sorry for scaring you."

Sarah snorted, the sound much louder than it needed to be. "Please. Takes more than a little panic attack to scare us." Her attempt at levity fell flat as she swayed. Clearly her night of drinking had an effect on her.

Isaac glared at Sarah, then cleared his throat. "Leah, you said you heard a voice? Did you recognize it?"

Leah shook her head. "I don't know. It was a woman's voice, calling for someone named Frank." She frowned, a nagging sense of familiarity at the name. "But... even hearing it felt wrong. Like I heard it in the Astral first, then here."

She trailed off, frustration building in her chest. Sarah squeezed her shoulder. "We can check with the Sages tomorrow. Maybe Eli or one of the other Sages will know something."

"Yeah, maybe," Leah said, not entirely convinced. She looked at the ruined walkie-talkie. "Whoever it is, they were calling for help."

CHAPTER 11

THE SCOUT

As dawn broke, Leah blinked away the remnants of sleep. Her heart sank as she saw her friends packing. She didn't need them to tell her they were preparing to leave for another mission.

Leah pushed herself up, watching them move about the tent with practiced efficiency.

"You need any help?" Leah asked, her voice still rough with sleep.

Sarah looked up, sporting a forced smile on her face. "Nah, we've got it. But if you grab us breakfast, I think we can eat before we head out."

Leah nodded, grateful for something to do. She slipped out of the tent, pulling her jacket tights around her as the cool morning air hit her. The camp was already stirring. A few Mystics nodded in her direction, but most kept their distance.

She returned with three steaming bowls of oatmeal, kicking the tent flap open with her foot. "Breakfast is served."

They ate in silence, Leah unsure of what to say. Sarah

was the first to break the quiet, her spoon clanking against the empty bowl.

"So, what's the plan while we're gone? More babysitting?"

Leah laughed. "I wouldn't call them babies, but yeah, more training. Someone's got to make sure they're ready."

Isaac nodded. "They're lucky to have you."

"I know." Leah sighed. "But I should be out there with you guys. Fighting."

The conversation lulled, and each became lost in their thoughts. Leah watched as her friends finished packing, her chest tightening with each passing moment. Finally, Sarah straightened up, slinging her pack over her shoulder.

"Well, I guess this is it," she said.

Leah stood, pulling Sarah into a tight hug. "Come back. Both of you. Don't do anything stupid."

Sarah laughed, the sound muffled against Leah's shoulder. "Me? Never."

They broke apart, and Leah turned to Isaac. He wrapped his arms around her and pulled her in.

"We'll be back before you know it," he murmured.

Leah nodded, not trusting herself to speak. As they pulled apart, she glimpsed something in Isaac's eyes—worry, maybe, or something else. But before she could puzzle it out, he looked away.

"Alright, enough of sappy shit," Sarah declared, squaring her shoulders. "We'll be back."

Leah followed as they stepped out of the tent, walking with them to the edge of camp where Zafirah and a group of White Knights waited.

"Take care," Leah said, her voice shaking.

Sarah grinned, punching Leah lightly on the arm. "Always do."

Leah watched as they disappeared into the forest. Long

after they'd vanished, she stood there, pulling her jacket tight around her.

Finally, she turned back to camp, squaring her shoulders. She had work to do.

The next few days passed in a blur of training sessions and sleepless nights. Leah threw herself into work, pushing her Squares harder than ever. If she had been busy enough, maybe she could have ignored the gnawing emptiness left by Sarah and Isaac's absence.

On the third day, Leah surprised her Squares. She'd borrowed some money from Eli, promising to pay him back. Flanked by a pair of White Knights, she walked into the local bakery. The warmth and the scent of fresh bread and caramelized sugar enveloped her.

"What can I get you?" the baker asked, eyeing her Mystic uniform warily.

Leah pointed to an assortment of pastries. "I'll take a dozen of those, please. And a dozen macaroons as well."

The baker's expression softened as he boxed up her order, turning to a smile as he took her money. Leah clutched the warm package to her chest as she returned to camp.

She found her Squares gathered near their usual training spot. Ricky sat with his back against a tree, no doubt still exhausted from the enhanced *Malchut* drills she had introduced to them yesterday. Beside him, Callum's gangly frame sprawled in the grass. His freckled face looked just like Sarah's after they pushed them too far. Even Ashley's boundless energy seemed dampened—she'd finally mastered the precision exercises, but her arms still trembled. Zoe lay on her stomach beside Ashley, chin propped in her hands, forming a small snowman. And Jenna, though she tried to hide it, could barely hold up her shoulders.

"Alright, everyone," Leah called out, holding up the box. "Consider this a reward for all your hard work lately."

Tired faces lit up as Leah passed out the fresh beignets and macaroons. Ricky actually smiled—a rare sight—while Callum practically inhaled his portion. Zoe sat up carefully, picking slowly at her pastry. Even Jenna, who tried to keep a distance from them, couldn't hide her smile as she accepted her share.

"These are amazing!" Ashley exclaimed. Powdered sugar dusted her chin as she devoured half her beignet.

For a moment, the weight on Leah's shoulders lifted. This was what she was fighting for, seeing this joy, free from death and carnage. These kids, despite everything, were growing stronger each day.

A shudder ran through her, tearing her away from this moment of peace to scan the tree line. Something felt off like eyes were watching her.

You're being paranoid, she thought. But the feeling lingered as she turned back to her Squares.

A week after Sarah and Isaac's departure, Leah led her Squares into the forest for their morning training. The air was even colder, biting deep into her bones. Their boots squelched in the mud as they reached a small clearing.

"Alright," Leah said, facing the group. "Today, we're going to work on the slashing *Malchut* technique we discussed last time. I want you to spread about six feet apart and choose a tree to practice on."

She watched as they took their positions. Ashley eyed the largest tree she could find—her typical of her eagerness to tackle the biggest challenge. Ricky tested the ground beneath him, settling into a solid. Zoe chose a smaller tree, shouldering up to Ashley as she muttered to herself about the best angle to cut.

"Remember, you're trying to create a blade of energy. Focus on narrowing your push," Leah said.

Whooshes of *Malchut* pushes filled the air, cracking bark and breaking branches. Each Square brought their own style to the technique, some refining what they'd practiced in hand-to-hand combat at the gym.

"Good work, Zoe." Leah watched as the small girl sent a precise slash of energy into her tree, the cut clean. "You've got a talent for this."

Zoe beamed at the praise, her usual quiet demeanor brightening as she redoubled her efforts.

Callum was next, his face scrunched up in concentration as he attempted the technique. His push was strong but unfocused, cracking the bark right off the trunk.

"Try to picture a thin line," Leah advised, flattening her hand and cutting through the air. "Channel your energy through that, just like when working the speed bag."

He nodded, taking a deep breath before trying again. This time, the cut was narrower, notching the trunk.

"That's it!" Leah grinned. "Keep practicing."

As she continued, Leah noticed Ashley helping a struggling Ricky refine his technique. But Leah's attention was fixed on Jenna, who stood apart from the others, her shoulders rigid. She hadn't even attempted the technique yet, just glaring at her tree as if it had offended her. Leah approached slowly.

"Everything alright?"

The girl looked at Lean, then back to the tree. "Fine," she muttered.

"You know, this isn't an easy technique," Leah said. "It's okay if you're struggling and need help."

"I said I'm fine."

Leah took a step back. She saw the defensiveness in Jenna's stance. It was the same stubborn pride she'd shown when they first found her, refusing help even when she clearly needed it. "Alright. Well, call on me if you need help."

She turned, watching Jenna as she moved to help Callum adjust his stance. As the morning wore on, the strange feeling of being watched returned. Leah looked around, noting how silent the forest was. No birds chirped, and no animals hopped out from their dens.

A chill swept through the space, blowing through Leah's jacket. She spun, her eyes landing on Jenna just as the girl unleashed a burst of energy. Something was wrong—the energy coming off her felt wild and uncontrolled.

The *Malchut* push tore through the air, far more substantial than it should have been, knocking her tree over. Jenna's eyes were wide as she turned to Leah, panic clear on her face as her pupils widened. Another wave of energy pulsed outward, causing a loud, concussive force.

"Everyone down!" Leah shouted, throwing herself between Jenna and the other Squares. Ashley moved toward Jenna, but Ricky grabbed her arm, pulling her behind a fallen tree. Zoe dropped instantly, pressing into the earth as Callum stumbled backward.

Leah pulsed a wave of *Malchut* back, neutralizing the attack. A cold bit down on her, frost building on her arm. The trees cracked and groaned around her as Jenna's pulses grew more erratic.

Jenna collapsed to her knees, her small frame shaking violently as she clutched her head. Dark veins spider-webbed across her temples as she let out a whimper that made Leah's heart clench.

"Jenna!" Leah called out, inching closer. "Jenna, I need you to focus on my voice. Can you hear me? Focus on my voice."

Another wave of energy lashed out, hitting Leah in the shoulder. She gritted her teeth against the pain and continued forward. Behind her, she heard Zoe's quiet voice counting breaths. Ashley whispered something while Ricky kept her from rushing forward.

"You've called on *Nehemoth*. I know those voices you hear are scary but listen to me. You can control this. Breathe. Let it go."

Jenna's eyes met hers. Frozen tears glistened on her face as her lips turned blue.

"That's it," Leah said. "Look at me. Stay with me. You've got this."

Leah took another step forward, pushing through the *Malchut* pulses. Finally, she reached her, wrapping her arms around the girl and pulling her close.

"You aren't alone. I've got you," Leah whispered.

Jenna's breath caught in her throat then relaxed into Leah's arms. Slowly, the pulses of energy subsided. The temperature returned, and Leah could hear the other Squares stirring behind her.

Jenna sagged against her, sobs wracking her small frame as tiny black veins spidered out from her temple. Leah held her tightly.

"That's it. Breathe."

"I'm sorry," Jenna choked out between sobs. "I'm so sorry."

Leah looked up, checking on the others. Ashley hovered

nearby while Ricky tried his best to hold her. They were all fine, with no injuries that she could see, but they were most definitely shaken.

"It's okay," Leah assured Jenna. "We're all okay." Leah stood, looking out to the others. "Why don't you all take a break? Get some water, catch your breath."

The Squares headed back up the path toward camp, Ashley looking over her shoulder while Ricky gently guided her. Zoe and Callum followed, their usual chatter replaced by silence.

Leah turned her attention back to Jenna. She stopped crying but kept looking back toward the trees, refusing to look at Leah.

"Do you want to talk about it?" Leah asked.

Jenna shook her head, then paused. "How did you know I was hearing voices?"

"Because I've been there, too," Leah admitted. "*Nehemoth* preys on people like us. But you aren't alone, I promise. Any time you need to talk, I'm here."

Jenna looked up at her, a flicker of hope in her eyes. "Really?"

Leah smiled. "Yes, really."

Jenna nodded, and her own small smile tugged at her lips. "Okay."

As Jenna opened her mouth to speak again, the moment was shattered when the rush of approaching footsteps sounded. Leah tensed, pushing Jenna behind her as she scanned the tree line.

Jaime emerged from the trees with a White Bishop at his side. His eyes blazed yellow as he looked around them.

"What happened?" he demanded. "We felt the energy spike from camp."

Leah straightened, keeping herself between Jaime and

Jenna. "Just a training accident. Everything's under control now."

Jaime's eyes narrowed, but movement caught his attention before he could press further.

A raven dove through the air above the clearing. The bird's flight pattern seemed wrong, too direct. Leah watched it bank sharply and circle back toward them. Beady eyes locked onto their group with a strange intelligence.

Jaime's hand flew to the sky, yellow eyes tracking the bird's movement. "Get down!" he roared, pointing his finger.

Leah didn't hesitate. She threw herself over Jenna, shielding the girl with her body as Jaime fired.

The *Malchut* bullet tore through the air, a concentrated burst of energy that caught the raven mid-flight. There was a sickening crunch of bone and a spray of dark blood as the creature plummeted to the ground.

For a moment, everything was still. Then, the raven's body twitched and convulsed, bones cracking and reforming as it grew larger.

Leah's stomach churned as she watched the transformation. Where the bird had fallen, the body of a teenage boy now lay, his arm a mangled mess of bone and sinew.

"Shifter." Jaime advanced on the creature with his finger trained on his head.

The boy's head snapped up, dark eyes fixing on Jaime. A grin spread across his face, revealing too-sharp teeth.

"Hello, Rook," he said in a raspy voice. "Your son sends his regards."

Jaime's face contorted with rage. He stomped down on the shifter's broken arm, eliciting a shriek of pain.

"How many more of you are out there?" he demanded.

The shifter's only response was to spit a glob of black blood at Jaime's feet.

Leah felt Jenna trembling against her as she watched the carnage unfold. She had to do something.

"Jaime," Leah called out, her voice steady. "We need to get this Square back with the others."

For a moment, Leah thought he hadn't heard her. Then he nodded sharply, not taking his eyes off the shifter.

"Bishop!" Jaime barked. "Escort her back and watch the others. Now!"

The White Bishop moved quickly, herding Jenna away from the clearing. Leah hesitated, torn between staying to help Jaime and returning to her Squares.

"Go," Jaime said, his voice leaving no room for argument. "I'll handle this."

Leah nodded, joining the Bishop and Jenna. As they reached the edge of the clearing, a wet, tearing sound made her turn.

The shifter had lunged at Jaime, his good arm elongating into long claws. But Jaime was faster. Three shots rang out in quick succession, and the creature fell, black blood pooling beneath his misshapen body.

Jaime stood over the boy, his chest heaving. Leah glimpsed him falter for a moment, his face softening and a pained look washing over him.

Then his eyes met hers, and the mask slipped back into place. "Go," he repeated. "I'll report this to the Queens."

CHAPTER 12

SHIFTERS

The antiseptic smell assaulted her senses as Leah guided the Squares into the makeshift hospital. The familiar scent transported her back to countless times spent in an infirmary, getting stitched up and poked with an IV.

A gray-haired medic with a thick mustache and wearing a Black Bishop cloak, crisp despite the early hour, ushered them inside. "This way." He gestured towards a row of examination rooms. "We'll get everyone checked out."

The Squares filed in, their earlier bravado replaced by nervous glances and hushed whispers. All except Jenna, who hung back, her eyes fixed on the scuffed linoleum floor. The black spidered veins on her temple were already receding, and *Nehemoth*'s corruption was already fading.

Leah crouched down, meeting the girl's gaze. "Hey," she whispered. "You okay?"

Jenna bit her lip, fighting back tears. "I could have killed them."

"You wouldn't be the first. My first time, I broke a girl's arm and nearly took out the rest of the Squares."

"No way." Jenna's eyes widened.

"Way," Leah said, briefly grinning before her smile vanished. "I'd just lost my parents, and I wasn't thinking right."

Jenna looked down at the ground and nodded.

"Well," Leah continued, "how about you go in and get checked out, okay?"

"Thanks," Jenna mumbled. "For everything."

Leah straightened, watching as Jenna disappeared into an examination room.

As much as I hate interrupting this touching moment, Asmodeus's voice cut through her thoughts. *We have bigger problems.*

Leah's eyes narrowed as she looked toward camp beyond the hospital. Something was wrong. Groups of Mystics rushed between tents, their movements urgent and coordinated. Leah called on *Tiferet,* her vision sharpening as she scanned the perimeter. Black Bishops and Knights had taken defensive positions, weapons drawn and eyes flashing yellow as they called on *Tiferet.*

Maybe they found more shifters, Leah thought.

She sprinted back towards where she'd left Jaime, her heart pounding in time with her footfalls. As she neared the clearing, the acrid smell of blood assaulted her nostrils.

Dozens of Black and White Bishops swarmed the scene while groups of Black Knights patrolled the perimeter. Sharp cracks far off in the woods set Leah's teeth on edge. No doubt bursts of *Malchut.*

In the center of it all stood Jaime, barking orders at a team dressed in full biohazard suits. His face was flushed, a vein pulsing at his temple as he gestured wildly.

"... wait until the blood dries out!" Jaime snapped, his Scottish brogue thickened by stress. "The blood's extremely contagious until it's dry. Stand guard until we can get a proper disposal team."

Leah had never seen him so agitated. She opened her mouth to speak, but another Black Knight beat her to it.

"Sir, no sign of another shifter," the Knight reported. "It seems this one was acting alone."

Jaime's *Tiferent* eyes flashed dangerously. "Keep looking. I want perimeter checks tripled."

"Yes, sir," the Knight replied, relaying the orders through his radio.

Jaime turned, spotting Leah. He strode towards her, his jaw clenched. "Walk with me," he said as he passed her by.

Leah fell into step beside him, matching his pace. "What's a shifter doing here? I thought we didn't need to worry about them this far north."

Jaime laughed. "I warned them they'd expand. No one wanted to believe me when I reported seeing one in Florida." He paused, tugging at the scarf around his neck. Leah spotted the silver chains beneath, holding his own infection at bay. "But a scout here, that's alarming, to say the least."

As they rounded a corner, the Victorian house where Leah had eavesdropped on the Queens' meeting came into view.

"Where are we going?" Leah asked.

"To tell that woman how much of an idiot she's been," Jaime growled.

Leah's steps faltered. "Should I be going? I don't think I'm qualified—"

Jaime whirled to face her. "You were a witness, and that shifter was hunting you and your Squares. I'd expect a little more fight in you."

He was right; she'd felt something watching them for weeks, waiting for the right time. She squared her shoulders. "Fine, let's go."

As they approached the house, two White Bishops moved to block their path.

"You can't come in," one said. "Queen's meeting in progress."

"Move aside," Jaime said.

The Bishops hesitated, but Jaime didn't wait for a response. He snapped his fingers, and both guards froze in place, their eyes wide as they were held by *Hod*.

"Come, Leah," he said, striding past the immobilized guards.

Leah followed, murmuring a quick "sorry" to the guards as she passed.

They burst into the living room, interrupting what appeared to be a heated discussion. Queen Micah was on his feet, his face flushed with anger. Jan Xie and Helen remained seated, their expressions a mix of surprise and annoyance.

"What is the meaning of this?" Micah demanded.

Jaime ignored him, his gaze locked on Jan Xie. "What are you doing here?"

Jan Xie's nostrils flared. "Not that it should concern you, but I am here on urgent business."

"Oh really?" Jaime's hands balled into fists. "Well, you know what concerns me? The fucking security of this place. I just neutralized a shifter scout."

Jan Xie shot to her feet, her chair scraping across the floor. "That's not possible," she hissed. "I burned them all before coming!"

"You what?" Jaime shouted.

"I killed them," Jan Xie spat back.

Leah finally took in the fresh cuts on Jan Xie's face and neck, the bandages around her hand, and the splints on three of her fingers—all clear evidence of a very recent and violent conflict.

The Black Queen narrowed her eyes at Leah. "You shouldn't be here, Knight. Get out."

Jaime stepped forward, placing himself between Leah and Jan Xie. "She's staying. She's a witness."

Jan Xie's jaw clenched. "Our safe house in Texas was compromised. We planned on bringing them here, but negotiations with the rootworkers were still underway. Before we could permit safe passage, shifters infected the place. We fled with the few Mystics we could before burning everything else down."

Leah pieced it all together, imagining what might have happened if that crow shifter had infected her or the Squares.

Jaime's shoulders relaxed. "I'm sorry," he said, his voice softer now. "How many casualties?"

"Under twenty," Jan Xie replied. "It was one of the smaller safe houses. But they were mostly younger Squares and Pawns."

Leah's stomach turned at the thought. Images of her own Squares ending up pale and still in hospital beds flashed through her mind. More children were dead because they weren't strong enough to protect them. Her fingers curled into fists at her sides, nails biting into her palms as she fought back the urge to scream.

"I sent a squad with Zafirah," Micah added. "They're scouting the area. Thankfully, the Shifters they've found have been of lower rank."

A crackle of static broke through the room, followed by a female voice from Jaime's radio.

"Rook McMillan, do you copy? The perimeter is clear. I repeat, the perimeter is clear."

"Thank God," Jaime murmured before responding. "Copy that. Continue monitoring. If you spot another one, notify me immediately and neutralize it."

"Copy that, sir."

Jaime tucked the radio away. "We'll keep an eye on it, but if we spot two or three more shifters, we've been compromised."

"Let's hope it doesn't get to that," Helen said as she eyed Leah.

"We should tell the rootworkers. They need to know," Leah said, the words tumbling out before she could stop them. All eyes in the room snapped to her.

"No," Jan Xie said. "They'd instruct us to leave by threat of war."

Leah frowned, meeting the Black Queen's gaze. "But we're here based on mutual trust. Madeline won't stop the 1891 from pushing us out if they find out."

"She has a point," Jaime said. "They no doubt heard us raiding the woods."

Micah sat in a chair at the head of the table, resting his elbows. "We wouldn't have anything to bargain. Just the hope that Madeline would take pity on us as she holds back the 1891."

"But we don't have to tell everyone," Leah said. "If we explain the situation to Madeline, I'm sure she'll understand."

"Why are we listening to this Black Knight?" Jan Xie asked with gritted teeth.

"I—"

Helen raised her hand, cutting off Leah's response. "That would be all, Leah," she said, her voice calm but firm. "Please get checked with a Medic. It sounds like you cut it close with the shifter."

Leah wanted to say more, but she saw the dismissal in Helen's gaze.

Jaime gave her a quick nod. "I'll take it from here, lassie. You got them to listen. Now go check on your Squares."

Leah stood at attention, turned on her heel, and marched out of the house.

"They still see me as a child," she grumbled. "A symbol when it's convenient, but not a voice worth hearing."

You're learning, Asmodeus murmured in her mind. *Politics is a game. Your time will come.*

Leah drew a deep breath. He was right, as much as she hated to admit it. This wasn't a battle she could win with force. She needed to be smarter and more strategic.

She walked into the hospital, spotting her Squares. They needed someone to speak for them, to protect them.

And Leah Ackerman, Black Knight and reluctant war hero, would be damned if she let them down.

CHAPTER 13
OLD INJURIES

Leah's boots scuffed against the floorboards as she walked around the makeshift hospital.

"Leah!" Nick's voice cut through her thoughts. He emerged from a nearby room. "I didn't expect to see you here."

She forced a smile. "Queen Helen's orders. Mandatory check because of the shifter incident."

Nick's eyes flashed yellow as he scanned her. "I thought they said no was exposed to the blood. Did you—?"

"No," Leah sighed. "But extra precautions for their precious hero."

"Ah, yeah, of course." Nick gestured towards an empty examination room. "Well, let's make sure you're alright."

As they entered the small space, Leah eyed the sparse furnishings—a threadbare cot without sheets, a rickety metal chair, and cabinets with peeling paint. The room felt claustrophobic, a far cry from the state-of-the-art medical facilities at HQ.

"Please, sit on the cot." Nick retrieved a stethoscope from a nearby drawer.

Leah perched on the edge of the thin mattress. She

watched Nick fumble with the stethoscope, nearly dropping it before placing it around his neck.

"Sorry," he muttered. "It's been a long day."

"I bet," Leah replied, her eyes drawn to the dark circles under Nick's eyes. "How have you been holding up?"

Nick paused, his hand hovering over a blood pressure cuff. "I'm managing. We all are, I suppose."

An awkward silence fell between them as Nick took her vitals. Leah became hyper-aware of every slight sound, from the soft whir of the blood pressure machine to Nick's breathing to the distant murmur of voices from beyond the thin walls.

"So," Nick said as he jotted down some numbers, "how are things with your Squares? I heard about the *Nehemoth* incident in the forest."

"They're fine. A little shaken up, but they'll be fine."

Nick nodded. "And you?"

Leah swallowed hard. She knew he could see past the barriers she'd built.

"I'm fine," she said. "Just doing my job, you know? Someone has to keep those kids safe."

Nick frowned. "It's okay to not be okay. After everything that's happened."

Images flashed through Leah's mind. Chaos at HQ, Gabe's last moments, the weight of the mandrake potion in her hands. She blinked rapidly, willing the memories away.

"I can't afford to fall apart," she whispered. "Too many people are counting on me."

Nick pulled the chair closer to the cot. "I understand that feeling too well. But bottling everything up doesn't help in the long run. Trust me, I know."

Leah looked up, surprised by the break in his voice. "What do you mean?"

Nick ran a hand through his hair. "I replay that night in

my head. If I'd been faster. If I'd noticed the signs earlier. Then maybe... maybe Gabe would still be here."

Hearing Gabe's name sent a jolt through Leah's chest. She gripped the edge of the cot, her knuckles turning white.

"It wasn't your fault," she said, the words feeling hollow even as she said them.

"It wasn't yours either," Nick countered.

Leah wanted to argue, but the words wouldn't come. Instead, a choked sob escaped her lips.

Nick leaned forward and grabbed her shoulder. "It's okay. Let it out."

And suddenly, the dam broke. Tears streamed down Leah's face as months of suppressed grief came pouring out. Her body shook with each sob, years of pain finally finding release.

"I see him everywhere," she gasped between sobs. "In my dreams, when I close my eyes. I thought I saw him at the bar the other night, just standing there with his stupid, messy hair. But he's gone, and I couldn't save him, and everyone keeps calling me a hero when I feel like such a failure."

Nick moved beside her on the cot, wrapping an arm around her shoulders. "You're not a failure, Leah. You did everything you could. We both did. Sometimes, we can't save everyone, no matter how much we want to."

Leah leaned into Nick's embrace, allowing herself to be comforted for the first time since that terrible night. "I miss him," she whispered.

"I know," Nick said.

They sat like that for a long moment. Leah felt the tension in her muscles unwind and the weight on her chest easing ever so slightly.

As her sobs quieted, Leah noticed a warmth spreading through her body. She pulled back slightly, looking at Nick.

"Are you using *Chesed?*" she asked.

Nick shook his head. "No. Just naturally warm. I thought about it, but sometimes the best healing comes from feeling the pain."

Leah nodded, wiping her eyes. "I've been trying so hard to be strong," she admitted. "To be the hero everyone needs me to be."

"Being strong doesn't mean never showing weakness. It means facing the pain and moving forward."

Leah laughed. "Even when I'm a sobbing mess?"

Nick chuckled. "Especially then."

She took another deep breath. "Thank you."

He flashed a warm smile. "Anytime."

Shouts sounded from outside the room, followed by a rush of footsteps racing past the door.

Nick stood and cracked the door open. "Looks like another patrol just got back." He turned to face her. "I should probably go see if they need help."

Leah nodded, rising from the cot. "Yeah, of course. Duty calls, right?"

Nick paused and looked at her as they made their way to the door. "Leah, please promise me you won't keep everything bottled up anymore. My door is always open if you need to talk about anything."

"Yeah. Yeah, I promise," Leah said.

And for the first time in a long while, she meant it.

Nick squeezed her shoulder gently before moving to the door. "Walk with me? I could use another set of hands."

Leah nodded, grateful for the chance to feel useful. As they stepped into the hallway, the chaos of the hospital wing surrounded them. White Knights rushed past with supplies while Black Bishops moved between rooms, their yellow *Tiferet* eyes scanning patients.

"Jan Xie's team got hit hard," Nick explained in a low

voice as they walked. "We've been getting survivors trickling in all morning."

Leah's throat tightened. More casualties in a war that seemed endless. They passed room after room of injured Mystics, some conscious and others deeply sedated. The antiseptic smell couldn't quite mask the underlying scent of blood and burned flesh.

Nick checked a chart, and Leah looked into an open doorway. Through it, she caught sight of a woman with curly blonde hair lying on a cot, her face achingly familiar despite the bandages covering much of her body. Though she was older, Leah recognized her face immediately.

"Anat," she breathed memories of Tom's past flooding her mind.

CHAPTER 14
PROMISES

"You know Jan Xie's right hand? How?" Nick frowned, following her gaze.

Leah's hands trembled as she gripped the door-frame, her mind reeling from the impossibility before her. "I don't exactly *know* her," she said. "But I know someone who does."

The room was dim, medical equipment steadily beeping as Anat lay still, her chest rising and falling in shallow breaths. Her face was exactly as she saw them in Tom's memories—though older now and marked by years of battle.

"She's been in a coma since they brought her back," Nick said softly. "Not sure what's keeping her under."

"I'll be right back," Leah said abruptly, turning to Nick. Her heart raced with possibility. After all this time, she could finally fulfill her promise to Tom. "Can you make sure no one moves her?"

"Sure, why?" Nick frowned. "Everything alright? You look like you've seen a ghost or something."

"You have no idea."

As Leah sprinted back to her tent, her mind raced. This was Anat, Tom's friend. After all this time, and all this searching, she could finally bring him to her. She found the book tucked away in the corner of her room, her hand shaking as she picked it up.

"Tom," she called. "I need to talk to you."

The air shimmered, and Tom's spectral form materialized before her. His boyish form folded his arms as he looked at her.

"What's wrong?" he asked, floating closer.

Leah took a deep breath. "I found her. I found Anat."

Tom's eyes widened. "You... you did? Is she okay?"

"She's alive, but..." Leah hesitated. "Something's wrong. She won't wake up. I can take you to her right now."

Tom's initial smile crumbled, his spectral form flickering as he wrapped his arms around himself. He drifted backward, his boyish features contorting with uncertainty. "But... I can't. I'm not ready. What if she doesn't recognize me? What if—"

"Tom, this is what we've been waiting for," Leah said. "This is your chance to find peace."

As the words left her lips, Asmodeus's presence surged within her, his voice a low growl in her mind.

Don't be a fool. We need him. You know what's at stake.

Leah gritted her teeth, pushing back against him. "This isn't about what we need," she hissed. "It's about doing what's right."

Tom looked between Leah and the empty air where Asmodeus's voice emanated. "What's going on?"

Leah forced a smile. "Nothing. Are you ready?"

Tom hesitated, then nodded. "Yes. Please take me to her."

Asmodeus continued to shout in her head as they hurried back to the hospital.

You're throwing away our advantage. Without his abilities, we'll be blind to dormant demons. You're putting everyone at risk.

Leah's steps faltered, doubt creeping in. She promised Tom. Was she making a mistake? They needed every advantage.

When they reached Anat's room, Leah closed the door behind them. Nick had already left, likely tending to the others. Looking at Anat now, Leah's chest tightened. The strong woman from Tom's memories lay broken before them, her body full of scars. Fresh bruises mottled her skin.

"Tom," Leah whispered, "are you ready?"

The ghost boy nodded, his eyes fixed on Anat's still form.

Leah took a deep breath and activated *Thagirion*, the familiar chill washing over her as she stepped into the first layer of the Astral.

The world took on a sickly yellow tinge, sounds muffling as if underwater. Tom's form became more solid, his features sharpening as he drifted towards Anat's bedside.

What Leah saw made her gasp. Anat's spirit hovered inches above her body, connected by thin threads that looked ready to snap. Whatever had happened to her nearly severed her connection to the physical world.

"Anat!" Tom rushed forward, his spectral hands passing through her floating form. "No, no, no..."

"Tom, wait—" Leah started, but it was too late.

The moment Tom touched Anat's spirit, corruption erupted in his form. His features twisted, teeth elongating as shadows writhed around him. But instead of attacking, he curled protectively around Anat's floating spirit.

"Won't let them take her!" he growled, his voice distorted. "Won't lose her again!"

"Tom, listen to me," Leah pleaded. "Maybe you can help her. You could guide her back."

The creature that had been Tom turned its blazing eyes on her. "Lies! Always lies!"

"No lies," Leah said, taking a careful step forward. "Look at her spirit, Tom. Look at those threads. She's not dead, just stuck. She needs help."

Tom's monstrous form shuddered. For a moment, his original shape flickered through. "Help... how?"

"I don't know. But she's your friend, right? Call her back, tell her you're here."

The shadows around Tom receded as he looked down at Anat's spirit. His clawed hands gentled as he reached for the gossamer threads.

"Anat," he whispered, his voice clearing. "It's me. It's Tom. Come back. I'm here."

Anat's spirit stirred, responding to his voice. The threads connecting it to Anat's body pulsed with soft light.

"That's it," Leah encouraged. "Keep talking to her."

Tom's form continued to shift between monster and boy as he spoke, telling Anat about all the years he'd waited, all the things he'd wanted to say. The threads grew stronger with each word, pulling her spirit back toward her body.

"I'm sorry I disappeared. I'm sorry I left you alone."

"Tom?" Anat's eyes fluttered open as they settled into her body, confusion giving way to shock as she took in the scene before her.

Tom froze, pulling back to look at her. "A-Anat?"

Tears welled in Anat's eyes as she struggled to sit up, wincing at the pain of her injuries. "Is it really you?"

The shadows surrounding Tom receded, his form solidifying into the familiar shape of the young boy. Tears streamed down his spectral cheeks.

"I... I thought you were gone," Tom choked out, his hand hovering just above Anat's.

Anat laughed, tears welling in her eyes. "I wouldn't leave without you, idiot."

Leah felt like an intruder witnessing their reunion. She backed away slowly, prepared to drop *Thagirion*, but Tom's voice stopped her.

"Leah," he called, his spectral form more solid than she'd ever seen. "Thank you for keeping your promise."

Leah's throat tightened as she saw him fading. "Tom..."

He smiled, his form growing transparent. "It's okay. I can go now. She's safe."

Before disappearing completely, he leaned down and whispered something in Anat's ear. Then he was gone, leaving only a sense of peace in his wake.

Leah dropped *Thagirion*, tears sliding down her cheeks as she watched Anat's eyes flutter open.

You've made us vulnerable, Asmodeus growled in her mind. *When people die because we can't detect dormant demons, remember this moment.*

"I will," Leah whispered, watching color return to Anat's cheeks. "And I'll remember that sometimes saving one person is worth more than any advantage."

She stepped out of the room as Nick rushed in to check on his now-conscious patient, knowing that Tom had finally found peace somewhere.

CHAPTER 15
AN OLD FRIEND

Leah's spoon clattered against her bowl as familiar voices cut through the cafeteria's usual drone. She froze, hardly daring to believe it. But there they were—Sarah and Isaac, supporting a figure between them. Emma hobbled forward on a wooden crutch, her movements stiff and careful. The three of them bore the marks of recent battle—in new uniforms that barely covered the bruises. But they were alive.

Her heart leaped into her throat as she pushed back from the table, chair legs scraping against the floor. She rushed towards them, her feet carrying her before her mind could fully process what she saw.

"Sarah! Isaac! You're okay!" As she drew closer, Leah saw the haunted look in their eyes, the way Sarah's shoulders sagged under an invisible weight. Isaac's usually pristine appearance was disheveled, his shirt stained with what looked disturbingly like dried blood.

And Emma.

Leah's breath caught as she took in the friend she hadn't seen since the trials. Emma's face was pale, with dark circles under her eyes that spoke to sleepless nights and horrors. Despite the healing all three must have already received, her right leg was heavily bandaged.

"Leah," Sarah managed a weak smile. "Good to see you."

Leah wrapped her arms around all three, careful not to jostle Emma. "What happened? Are you okay?"

Isaac let out a humorless chuckle. "Define 'okay.'"

"The medics did what they could," Emma said, adjusting her grip on the crutch. "But they said the bone needs time to set. But even with *Chesed*, this leg isn't doing me any favors."

Leah nodded, guiding them to her table. As they settled in, she couldn't help but notice Sarah's eyes scanning the room, assessing the exits. Isaac's hand drifted to his side as if reaching for a weapon that wasn't there.

"Do you want food? I'll grab some food," Leah offered, desperate to do anything to help.

As she turned to leave, Sarah caught her wrist. "I'll go with you. You'll need the extra hands."

Leah caught sight of her friend's eyes. She nodded, walking beside Sarah toward the makeshift buffet line where camp workers had set out metal trays of food on folding tables. She glanced back at Emma before turning to the steaming serving stations.

Sarah took a deep breath as they reached the buffet line. "It's Harry," she said. "He... he didn't make it."

Leah's stomach turned, and she gripped the edge of the metal table. "What?"

Sarah sniffled. "The shifters got him. I found the body. Emma was there, too. Saw it happen."

Memories of Harry surfaced. His infectious laugh, terrible jokes, how he'd try to make light of any situation. Now gone. Just like that.

"How—" Leah started, her voice failing her. She swallowed hard, forcing the words out. "How many more can we afford to lose?"

Sarah gripped Leah's arm. "We don't have a choice. We keep fighting."

Leah nodded, blinking back tears. Sarah squeezed her arm again. "I needed to tell you before... you know. Makes it easier if you know going in."

They rejoined the group carrying trays of food. Leah's heart ached as she saw Emma staring blankly at the table. They all picked at their trays, no one particularly hungry.

Leah glanced at Emma, wanting to ask about everything but unsure where to start. "I heard you were tracking something in Japan before everything went sideways. What happened out there?"

Emma looked up and blinked, a slight smile forming on her face. "We were. These spirits, called tengus, were snatching kids in the woods. Ended up being one of the bigger ones, a hanadaka tengu from the mountains."

As Emma recounted the investigation into a destroyed shrine and a massive forest, Leah saw some tension leaving her shoulders. The pain was still there, lingering just beneath the surface.

"And then?" Leah prompted gently when Emma fell silent.

Emma's face darkened. "And then everything went to hell. The tengus can teleport, so we lost the damn thing. Then, the shifter activity in Venezuela spiked. Next thing I know, I'm hip-deep in the jungle. It sucked. Nearly every mission, I was the least prepared."

Sarah reached out, squeezing Emma's hand. "I heard the reports. You did better than you think you did," she said. "Better than any of us could have done."

Emma scoffed, looking up at the ceiling. "Fat lot of good it did in the end."

A silence fell over the table. Leah cleared her throat, about to ask another question, but Isaac cut in.

"What about you, Leah? Did anything exciting happen around here while we were gone?"

"Well," she started, "there was this one incident with a shifter scout—"

She was cut off by a sudden, piercing voice in her head. "Leah."

Leah jumped, her knee banging against the table. The voice was masculine and all too familiar.

"You okay?" Sarah asked, looking around the hall for danger.

"I'm fine," Leah managed, rubbing her temples. "Just Eli, apparently sending telepathic messages now instead of using a damn radio."

Eli's monotone voice filled her mind again. "We've been cleared to start joint training with the rootworkers. You'll represent the Infinity Board starting tomorrow evening. Take Isaac and Sarah with you."

"What does he want?" Isaac asked.

"He's cleared us for training in town tomorrow," she said.

"Training? With the rootworkers?" Emma's eyes widened. "Is that safe?"

Leah sighed, leaning back in her chair. "Safe? Probably not, but we've already got Squares training with their kids. This is just another necessary step to make any headway with them."

Isaac leaned forward. "And it's an opportunity for us to get intel."

Sarah's eyes narrowed. "Or, we're all about to walk into a trap."

CHAPTER 16

BOXING MATCH

The streets of the Sekrè Fami were quiet, save for the occasional creak of a snow-laden branch or the distant bark of a dog. Leah walked between Sarah and Isaac, their footsteps crunching fresh snow as they made their way to the boxing gym.

"Remember when we had that massive snowball fight at the Academy?" Sarah asked, her eyes scanning the snow-covered rooftops.

Isaac chuckled, the sound warming the cold air. "How could I forget? You pelted me so hard I had bruises."

"Not my fault you're such an easy target," Sarah teased, taking a swing at his shoulder.

Leah grinned but kept her eyes ahead. Something felt off about this whole situation. The streets were too empty, the air too charged with tension. She couldn't shake the feeling they were walking into something far different from the joint training session they'd been told to expect.

"Everything alright?" Isaac asked.

"I don't know," Leah admitted. "Something feels off."

As they rounded the corner, the boxing gym came into view. Leah stopped in her tracks, taking in the scene before her. At least fifty rootworkers crowded the entrance, far more than the dozen or so she'd expected for a training session. The mass of bodies pressed against each other, some even perched on nearby stoops to get a better view. The air buzzed with anticipation, appearing more like a prizefight than a friendly sparring match.

"What the hell?" Sarah muttered.

Leah's stomach churned as they approached. She caught snippets of conversation from the gathered rootworkers, their words setting her nerves on edge.

"...teach those Mystics a lesson..."

"...put them in their place..."

"...show them what real power looks like..."

Isaac gently squeezed Leah's shoulder. "We don't have to do this. We could turn back."

But Leah knew they couldn't. Whatever was happening here, they needed to face it head-on. She squared her shoulders and pushed through the crowd, Sarah and Isaac close behind.

The interior of the gym was a cacophony of noise and movement. At least a hundred rootworkers were packed inside, filling the makeshift wooden stands lining the walls. More bodies pressed in behind them as the crowd from outside filed in, doubling the number. The air was already thick with body heat and tension. In the center of it all stood Mark, a grin on his face as he collected money and handed out betting slips.

"What's going on?" Leah asked. "This isn't a training session."

Mark smiled as he turned to the audience. "Ah, our guests of honor have arrived! Welcome, welcome. We've got quite the show planned for you today."

Leah clenched her hands into fists. "This isn't what we were told was happening. We didn't agree to this."

Mark shrugged. "Plans change. The people want to see what you Mystics are made of. Who am I to deny them?" The smug grin that covered his face only fueled Leah's anger.

Before Leah could respond, a commotion near the ring caught her attention. Claude made his way through the crowd, wearing boxing shorts, boxing shoes and a hoodie. His eyes locked onto Leah as a toothy grin spread across his face.

He pulled his hood down, and Leah noticed his wrapped hands. "The famous Leah Ackerman," he sneered, his voice carrying over the crowd's noise. "The Jew who thinks she can just waltz into our town and take it over."

Memories flooded over Leah, taunts and slurs from school rushing back to her. She felt Sarah tense beside her, ready to leap to her defense, but Leah held up a hand. She wouldn't give Claude the satisfaction of seeing her rattled.

Claude turned to the crowd and yelled, "It's time you Mystics get taught a lesson about respect."

The gym erupted in cheers, the voices bouncing off the walls, drowning Leah and her friends. Her mind raced, trying to process the situation. This wasn't just a rigged match—it was a deliberate attempt to humiliate her and break the fragile alliance between Mystics and rootworkers. That's why Claude was here when they first came to the gym. And based on the looks exchanged between Mark and some other organizers, this had been planned from the beginning.

As if confirming her suspicions, Eli's voice suddenly echoed in her mind as he sent her a telepathic message. "I'm sorry, Leah. The Board knew about this. They... we thought it might be a necessary step to solidify our position here."

She clenched her jaw. The Board betrayed her. Her leaders, the people she trusted, used her as a pawn. Anger heating her neck and threatening to overwhelm her.

"Leah?" Sarah's voice cut through the haze. "What's wrong?"

Leah blinked, forcing herself to focus. She couldn't fall apart now, not with so much at stake.

"Nothing," she lied. "Let's just get this over with."

As they were led to a corner to prepare, Leah caught sight of a familiar face in the crowd. Nykima sat alone, her wheelchair set off to the side of the stands. Their eyes met, and Nykima gave an almost imperceptible nod as if giving Leah a small show of support.

A gruff man in a stained tank top showed them to a cramped locker room that reeked of sweat and leather. Leah's hands trembled slightly as Sarah helped wrap them —not from fear, but from the strangeness of it all. She'd sparred countless times at the academy and outpost, but this was different. The wraps felt too tight, too restrictive compared to the freedom she was used to in combat.

"Remember to pivot on your back foot when you throw a cross." Sarah instructed, demonstrating the proper stand.

Leah nodded, testing her wrapped hands with a few practice jabs. The movements felt familiar yet foreign, like speaking a language she'd only read in books. Her stomach twisted as she remembered what Eli had said, wondering if she was walking right into another trap.

A faint tingling sensation spread up her arms when she slipped on the boxing gloves, like pins and needles, after sleeping wrong. She called on *Malchut*, but the familiar pressure in her chest slipped away.

"The gloves," she whispered to Sarah. "They're enchanted. I can't use *Malchut*."

Sarah frowned. "They're trying to weaken you."

Leah's throat tightened. Without access to her wells,

she'd have to rely purely on strength—strength that was already being drained away. Against Claude, she'd be at an even greater disadvantage than she'd thought. She'd essentially be fighting with one arm tied behind her back, getting weaker with every punch she threw.

"Make sure Isaac knows," she managed. "We need to be ready for anything."

The crowd's roar washed over her as Leah stepped into the ring. Claude stood in the opposite corner. Without his hood, Leah could see his muscles and toned shoulders. Fit was an understatement.

A thin man with a badly scarred face and crooked nose stepped between the two, wearing what looked like a referee's shirt. His bloodshot eyes darted between them as he mumbled through the rules, his words slurred as if he'd already been drinking. This wasn't an official overseeing a match—this was just another piece in their carefully orchestrated humiliation.

But Leah barely heard him. Her focus was entirely on Claude, on the hatred burning in his eyes.

The bell rang, its harsh clang echoing through the gym. Claude charged forward like a bull, his feet thundering against the canvas. Leah ducked and weaved, her smaller size allowing her to evade the initial onslaught. She caught glimpses of the crowd as she moved—some leaning forward, others already holding up their betting stubs.

She spotted an opening and landed a few quick jabs, but each impact sent a jolt of energy draining from her arms. It felt like trying to punch through water, her strength seeping away with every hit.

"That all you got, Jew?" Claude taunted, his words dripping with venom. Spittle flew from his lips as he advanced. "Thought your people were stronger than that."

Leah gritted her teeth. A memory surfaced—her

mother, talking to her after another incident at school. "Our strength isn't in our fists. It's in our hearts, in our minds. They can throw all the hate they want at us, but we stand tall."

Sarah shouted about the crowd. "Come on, Leah! You got this!"

Leah squared her shoulders. She advanced, channeling years of combat training into a solid combination—jab, cross, hook. Each punch landed with heavy thuds that drove Claude back. His eyes widened as he stumbled against the ropes. For a moment, the crowd's bloodthirsty cheers stopped. Leah caught Mark's face in the crowd, his smirk wavering.

The gloves' magic worked relentlessly. Each strike draining more energy, like poison spreading through her veins. She slowed; her reactions dulled. The ring seemed to tilt and sway, and Leah found herself watching the fight as if from above—seeing her own body struggle to maintain its guard.

Claud's lips curved into a cruel smile as he recognized the gloves taking effect. He unleashed a barrage of jabs, each one finding its mark. Leah tried to block, but her arms felt like lead weights. Pain exploded across her face as a right hook connected with her jaw. The impact sent her staggering, copper flooding her mouth as her teeth cut into her cheek.

Through the haze of pain, she forced herself to look at the crowd. Rootworkers pressed against the ropes, their faces eager for her defeat. Some shouted slurs that made her stomach turn. Sarah and Isaac stood helpless in the corner, their hands gripping the ropes so tight their knuckles had gone white. And there, in the back, she spotted several high-ranking Mystics, their faces carefully blank as they watched their war hero falter.

As Leah's knees buckled, understanding hit harder than any of Claude punches. They knew she'd lose. They knew about the enchanted gloves. The Board had orchestrated this entire humiliation. But why? They wouldn't risk their symbol of hope just to—

Then, even as her vision blurred, it dawned on her. This wasn't about humiliation. This was calculated. If even their war hero could fall, if the mighty Mystics showed weakness, perhaps the people of this town might take pity on them. Perhaps they'd let them stay.

With the last of her strength, Leah straightened her back and met Claude's gaze. The man's face was flushed with triumph as he wound up for the final blow. Leah wouldn't go down cowering. She'd face this with all the dignity and strength her mother had taught her.

She didn't have to wait long. The last punch came like a thunderclap, Claude's glove filling her vision. Then darkness rushed in, and Leah fell into the void.

CHAPTER 17

THE VOICE

Claude's fist hurtling towards her burned in Leah's mind as she lay on a cold, hard surface. As her consciousness came back to her, the scent of mold and decay filled her nostrils. She winced, tasting blood in her mouth.

Leah opened her eyes, adjusting to the yellow light permeating the ceiling. She pushed herself up on her elbows, wincing at the ache in her body. As her vision cleared, she realized she was still in the boxing gym, but it was empty.

The walls, which were pristine moments ago, were now covered in a thick layer of yellow moss creeping through the cracks. The ceiling sagged on one side, filled with dark, viscous water damage. Leah studied the room, taking in the warped floorboards and rusted equipment scattered about.

A wave of vertigo washed over her as she pushed herself to her feet. She stumbled, catching herself on the edge of the boxing ring. That's when she saw it—her own body, lying motionless on the canvas just a few feet away.

Leah's breath caught in her throat. She'd been in the Astral realm before, but only either in dreams or with her

115

complete physical form. She shook as she approached her unconscious body, noting the bruises already forming on her face and the stillness of her chest.

"Am I… dead?" she whispered, reaching out to touch her shoulder. Her body's eyes opened and vanished from Leah's sight.

"Not dead," a familiar monotone voice answered. "Just temporarily displaced."

Leah whirled around to find Eli standing behind her, his white Rook's cloak pristine even in this decayed reality. His face was impassive as ever, but something in his eyes made Leah's stomach churn with unease.

"Eli? What's going on? How did I end up here?"

Eli's gaze swept across the ring, settling on faintly glowing markings etched into the canvas. "They're clever," he murmured, more to himself than to Leah. "They modified the ring to cut off access to the Tree of Life. And if I'm not mistaken…" He reached down, prodding one of the boxing gloves from Leah's motionless hands. "These gloves are enchanted as well. Designed to drain your energy."

"Didn't you know that already?" Leah asked.

Eli met her stare, his expression unreadable. "We knew they were going to make a spectacle but only suspected there might be… complications."

Leah narrowed her eyes. "Complications? Is that what you call this? What was the point of humiliating me in front of everyone?"

"It was a calculated risk," Eli replied. "We needed to gauge the rootworker's capabilities to see how far they were willing to go."

Heat crept up Leah's neck. "By using me as bait? As some kind of sacrificial pawn?"

"You're not just any pawn, Leah," Eli said. "You're our

symbol. Sometimes, symbols need to fall so they can rise again stronger."

"So that's all I am?" she whispered. "A symbol to be manipulated and discarded?"

Eli shook his head. "We're fighting a war. Sometimes difficult choices have to be made for the greater good."

Leah opened her mouth to argue back, but before she could, a burst of static filled the air. She covered her ears, the sound growing louder.

"What the hell is that?" Eli asked looking left and right as he plugged his ears.

Leah's heart raced. She knew that sound. It was the same static she'd been hearing for weeks, the mysterious noise haunting her dreams. But here, in the Astral realm, it was clearer. Louder.

"You hear it, too?" Leah asked.

Eli frowned and nodded.

Leah pointed towards a decrepit speaker system hanging from the wall. "It's coming from over there."

As they approached, the static quieted. Snippets of words were spoken clearly through the speaker.

"...help...Frank..."

Leah froze. That voice. It sounded familiar.

"Cora? High Priestess?" she breathed.

Eli kneeled toward the speaker, inspecting it. "That's not possible."

Leah sided up to the speaker, pressing her ear against it. "Cora? Is that you? It's me, Leah. Can you hear me?"

The static intensified, and then...

"Leah? Leah Ackerman?"

Leah's knees nearly buckled with relief. "Yes! Yes, it's me! What happened? We thought Legion killed you all."

"I don't... time," Cora's voice crackled through the speaker. "Listen. Legion... he's not... what you think. The attack was not what it seemed. You need to find us. You need to—"

The connection cut out abruptly, replaced by a high-pitched whine that sent Leah jumping backward. She pounded on the speaker, desperate to reestablish contact. "Cora! Cora, come back! Where are you? How can I find you?"

But there was nothing but silence.

She turned to Eli, her mind racing. "We have to do something."

"But there's nothing to do," Eli said. "The Astral Witches are dead. Legion killed them."

CHAPTER 18

THE FATE OF THE WITCH

"Dead? What do you mean?" Leah's voice rose. "You just heard her! She needs our help!"

Eli crossed his arms. "Yet Legion couldn't have attacked HQ if they were still alive. The witches would have sensed them coming through the Astral and stopped the demons."

Leah shook her head. "Unless the demons did something first."

"I sent a squad after," Eli replied. "They found the tattoo parlor ransacked. Powerful magic had been used there."

"But did you find bodies? Any actual proof they're dead?"

Eli shook his head. "No. Legion doesn't leave bodies behind."

"So, you don't know if they're dead!" Leah shouted. "Why can't you hear yourself right now? Shouldn't we at least consider this?"

"Leah," Eli sighed, lowering his voice, "their sole purpose was to protect the Astral Realm. A crack between dimensions large enough for an army of demons to pour through can only mean one thing."

Leah put her arms out. "Then how do you explain what we just heard? Why would she say she's trapped if she were a ghost?"

"I... I don't know," he admitted after a long pause. "But It's possible Legion is luring you. Using voices of people you trust against you."

Leah pressed her lips, shaking her head. "No. That doesn't add up. She was calling for someone named Frank. Not me. I just ended up answering."

"We don't have the resources to hunt this down. We're spread too thin as it is."

"Then send me!" Leah said, grabbing Eli's arm. "I'll go alone if I have to."

Eli stared at her for a long while, then sighed. "I'll see what I can do." He touched her shoulder and pushed. But for now, you need to return to your body. You've been out far too long."

Leah opened her mouth to argue more, but a wave of dizziness washed over her. The gym around them blurred and faded.

"We'll discuss this more at camp," Eli said, his voice dissipating.

Cold reality slammed into Leah. She was standing, her hands balled into fists around her boxing gloves. She blinked, disoriented, as her senses slowly readjusted.

The first thing she noticed was the silence. The crowd's roar that had filled the gym moments ago was gone, replaced by a tense hush.

As her vision cleared and she looked down, Leah saw Claude.

The man lay motionless, his face a mess of bruises and swelling. Blood trickled from his nose, which looked crooked.

"Leah!" Sarah's excited voice cut through the silence. "That was incredible!"

Leah turned to see her friends beaming at her from ringside. The rest of the crowd remained quiet; shock evident on their faces.

"What…" Leah started her raspy voice barely above a whisper, a stabbing pain clawed her throat.

I might be upset with you, Asmodeus's voice echoed in her mind, *but no one insults us and then knocks us out like that.*

"What did you do?" Leah asked, careful to keep her voice low enough that only he could hear.

I taught him some respect, Asmodeus replied.

"But how?" Leah's eyes darted between Claude's prone form and the stunned onlookers. "He was so much stronger than us, and we didn't have energy."

Leah could feel Asmodeus's mental shrug. *He cut you off from the Tree of Life. But the Tree of Death was up for grabs. So, a little Gamaliel to confuse him and a calculated Nehemoth to throw him off was enough.*

"Well," Leah whispered, looking down at the Claude as he rolled over. "Thank you."

Before Asmodeus could respond, Mark's voice rang out. "Leah Ackerman is the winner."

He grabbed Leah's wrist, raising her arm in a half-hearted victory salute. The crowd let out a cheer, albeit more performative than anything.

"That was amazing!" Isaac said as he and Sarah climbed onto the stage.

Sarah punched Leah's shoulder. "For a second there, I thought you were dead."

Leah caught sight of Nykima passing by. The former Knight's lips pressed into a thin line, but something flickered in her eyes as she watched Leah—a mix of pride and worry that vanished as quickly as it appeared.

Mark's booming shouted behind her. "Who's ready for the second fight?"

A cheer rippled through the crowd, the shock of Claude's defeat giving way to bloodlust for the next match. Leah's eyes narrowed as she scanned the ring. Claude was gone, but his enchanted gloves lay discarded in the corner.

Something snapped inside Leah. She was tired of being manipulated, tired of half-truths and hidden agendas.

Without thinking, Leah thrust out her arm. A slice of *Malchut* flew out of her hand, slicing through the boxing ring floor. The cut was clean and precise, revealing the glowing markings etched into the wood beneath.

The crowd gasped, conversations dying mid-sentence as all eyes turned to her.

Mark whirled to face her, glaring. "What the hell do you think you're doing?"

Leah met his gaze. "If you want to put together a boxing match and run bets on us, fine. But if you're going to rig it and put us at a disadvantage, then we're done." She pointed at the exposed markings. "You see this? These symbols were meant to drain my power."

"What does she mean by rigged?" a voice shouted from the crowd.

The room erupted in overlapping voices. Some members of the 1891 faction pushed forward, faces twisted in anger, while others backed away, muttering among themselves.

Mark raised his hands, but sweat beaded on his forehead. "I have no idea what she's talking about."

"Liar." Leah's voice cut through the chaos. She turned to address the crowd directly, her finger still pointing at the exposed markings. "This mat had symbols to drain me and strengthen my competitor. Claude knew exactly what he was walking into."

The revelation caused an immediate chaos. Betting slips waved in the air as some spectators demanded their bets back. Others surged forward, shouting accusations at Mark. A chair crashed to the ground as someone hurled it in his direction.

"We're done here," Leah declared, stepping down from the ring. She caught Sarah and Isaac's eyes through the growing mayhem. "Come on. We need to find Eli."

CHAPTER 19

COMPROMISES

As Leah trudged back to camp with Sarah and Isaac, her muscles ached, the adrenaline from the boxing match fading to leave behind exhaustion.

"I still can't believe you took down that mountain of a woman," Sarah said, practicing her punches as they walked. "And the look on Mark's face when you cut through that ring? Priceless."

Leah managed a weak smile, but Isaac stayed quiet, his head down as they walked.

"What is it?" Leah asked, nudging his shoulder.

He sighed. "Asmodeus winning the fight will cause some trouble."

"Trouble?" Sarah scoffed. "Those assholes rigged the match! They deserved what they got."

"And now we've pissed off our allies," Isaac countered.

"I didn't know they were going to do that," Leah muttered. "I don't blame Asmodeus for sticking up for me."

Sarah glared at Isaac. "Yeah, and we're supposed to let them walk all over us? No way."

"I know, but now what happens?" Isaac asked. "They

barely tolerate us now. This could be the excuse the 1891 faction needs to push us out entirely."

Leah opened her mouth to respond, but movement at the edge of camp caught her eye. Eli, wearing a pristine white cloak, strode purposefully towards them.

"Leah," Eli said. "A word, if you please."

"What is this about?" Sarah asked, stepping forward.

Eli kept his gaze on Leah. "I've received a formal complaint from the rootworkers regarding the incident at the boxing gym. The Queens request your presence immediately."

Leah's throat tightened. She'd known there would be consequences, but this soon?

"Bullshit," Sarah growled. "They're the ones who rigged the match!"

"Sarah," Isaac warned, pulling her back.

Eli remained maddeningly neutral. "This incident will be discussed with the appropriate parties in attendance. Leah, if you'll come with me."

"It's okay," Leah said. "I'll catch up later."

She fell into step beside Eli, walking with him toward the makeshift Queen's headquarters.

"I don't know what you expected," Leah said. "The match was rigged, and Asmodeus was protecting me."

A muscle in Eli's jaw twitched. "Sometimes maintaining peace requires... compromises."

"Compromises," Leah echoed. "Is that what we call it when they try humiliating us?"

They reached the weathered Victorian house, and Eli paused at the door, his hand on the knob.

"For what it's worth," he whispered, "I believe Asmodeus did what he thought was right. But there are still consequences."

Before Leah could respond, Eli opened the door and

ushered her inside. They made their way down the narrow hallway. Eli knocked on a door at the end, and Leah's heart hammered in her chest as a muffled voice bid them enter.

White Queen Micah sat behind a battered desk, his salt-and-pepper hair more disheveled than usual. Dark circles shadowed his eyes. He looked up as they entered, his gaze settling on Leah.

"Please, have a seat," Micah said, his tone light.

Leah perched on the edge of a worn armchair. Eli remained at the door, standing guard.

"I assume you know why you're here," Micah continued, steepling his fingers.

Leah lifted her chin. "Because I exposed a rigged match, and Asmodeus and I refused to be played?"

Micah's eyebrow arched. "Still seeing it all for face value, I see. I expected better of you. From where I'm sitting, you've single-handedly jeopardized months of negotiations for your pride."

"With all due respect, sir," Leah said, struggling to keep her voice even, "how can we let them treat us like that?"

"So, the appropriate response is to humiliate their champion and destroy their property?" Micah's voice sharpened. "Did you consider, for even a moment, the effects of your actions?"

Leah's cheeks burned. "I was defending myself! Defending all of us!"

"Your actions were reckless," Micah countered. "I expected better of you. And now *we* are left to clean up the mess."

The air in the room seemed to thicken, pressing down on Leah's chest. She gripped the arms of the chair, her knuckles turning white.

"Okay, so, what now?" Leah hated how small her voice sounded.

Micah leaned back, his chair creaking. "Now, we do damage control. Madeline has requested you come to her side willingly until the matter is resolved. You'll remain under her supervision for the foreseeable future."

Leah frowned. "So, you're handing me over? Like some kind of prisoner?"

"It's that or lose our encampment," Micah said.

Leah's stomach churned, and she resisted the urge to vomit. "But... what about my Squares? My duties here?"

"Others will take over." Micah's expression softened. "I know this won't be easy, Leah. But if you go willingly, maybe you can get some more intel we can work with."

"But what about Legion? We don't have time for these games!"

"Enough," Micah said, standing and peering down at Leah. "You are to be in Madeline's possession immediately."

Leah opened her mouth to argue further, but the words died in her throat as the room blurred and faded. A moment of vertigo, and then—

She blinked, disoriented, as her surroundings solidified into a small, windowless room. A single fluorescent bulb buzzed overhead, casting shadows across the bare walls. A narrow cot with a thin mattress occupied one corner, and a door to what she assumed was a tiny bathroom stood opposite.

Panic clawed at her chest as the reality of her situation sank in. She was trapped. Confined. A prisoner.

Leah's fists clenched at her sides, energy surging through her veins as she fought the urge to lash out. To tear down these walls with her bare hands if necessary. But what would happen to their encampment if she tried to free herself? They needed to face Legion, but they were nowhere near ready.

She held back a scream, holding back her energy as she whirled around and let her fist connect with the wall. Drywall crumbled beneath her knuckles, leaving a small, satisfying hole.

Better? Asmodeus's dry voice cut through her rage.

Leah closed her eyes, exhaling slowly as she threw herself onto the cot. She let herself fall into darkness, and when she opened her eyes again, she was seated at the familiar round table in their shared mental space. Asmodeus sat across from her, pouring tea into delicate porcelain cups.

"Our leaders have no sense of dignity," he said, sliding a cup towards her.

Leah wrapped her hands around the warm ceramic, inhaling the soothing scent of chamomile. "Definitely not for anyone they control."

Asmodeus sipped his tea, his starry eyes studying her over the rim of his cup. "Strange, after all this time, that the Infinity Board still can't find Legion."

Leah nodded, considering his words. "You're right. He was injured. We should have been able to track him, even with Nona at his side."

"Unless more people were still pulling the strings," Asmodeus said. "Legion is without his shield conjurer. Any step he takes now would need to be slow and calculated."

"But we don't even know what he wants."

Asmodeus's gaze grew distant. "He wants to consume. He drained the Valley dry before coming here. No doubt he wants to do that here. But he'd need to get through the Mystics first."

A voice echoed through their shared mindscape. "Leah, can you hear me?"

Leah stood, frowning as she looked around the mental space. "Eli? What do you want?"

"I wanted you to know I put in your request. The one to go check on the Immortal Witches' Tattoo Parlor."

Leah's heart leaped. "And?"

"It got denied," Eli said. "The reports all claim the space is too dangerous to be visited. They can't dedicate enough resources."

"Not even if I went alone?" Leah asked. "If there is anything there, anything that can help us, then we have to check it."

"I think you can already see the Queens' stance on you going."

"Why don't they understand?" Leah shouted.

"They fear it's a trap set by Legion to lure you," Eli replied. "I'm sorry, Leah, I tried—"

"Fuck off, Eli."

The connection severed, leaving Leah alone with Asmodeus once more. She slumped back into her chair, running a hand through her hair.

Asmodeus leaned forward. "I'm sorry, but how long will we let the Board make decisions for us?"

Leah slammed her hand on the table. "It's like they don't want to find him."

A sound from the physical world intruded on their mental space—keys rattling. Leah opened her eyes, finding herself back in the cell. The door swung open, and a broad-shouldered man in a leather jacket stepped in, wearing a small Voodoo doll necklace.

"Come with me," he said gruffly. "Madeline is waiting."

CHAPTER 20
IN THE SHADOWS

"And if I refuse?" Leah asked as she looked up at the man holding her cell door open.

The man's eyes narrowed. "Then I drag you. Your choice."

Leah clenched her jaw but followed him out of the cell. As they descended a narrow staircase, the scent of lavender permeated the air. The fragrance grew stronger with each step until they passed through the bar of Le Syndicat.

They descended another set of stairs, heading deeper into the bowels of the bar. The walls closed in, and Leah felt like she couldn't breathe.

When she thought she couldn't take another step, they emerged into a dimly lit hallway. Ahead, she saw two familiar faces and furrowed her brow.

"Sarah? Isaac? What are you doing here?"

Her friends raced toward her, ignoring the man beside her and looking her over.

"Are you okay?" Sarah whispered.

"They wouldn't tell us where you went," Isaac said. "They just sent us here."

"Enough chatter. Keep moving," Leah's escort said.

As they rounded a corner, Leah saw a familiar figure in a wheelchair blocking their path.

"Nykima?" Leah said.

"I'll take them from here," Nykima told the man.

The escort shook his head. "I have orders to bring them directly to Madeline."

Nykima glared at him. "And I'm telling you, as the granddaughter of Madeline, that I'll take it from here."

After a long moment, the escort grunted in frustration and stormed off, leaving them alone with Nykima.

"What's going on?" Leah demanded. "Why are we here?"

Nykima rolled ahead, waving them on. "Not here. Follow me."

She led them to a small library. As soon as the door closed behind them, Nykima approached to face Leah.

"Tell me everything," she said with an urgency in her voice. "What happened in the Astral realm during the fight? What did you see?"

Leah's mind reeled, struggling to keep up. "How did you—"

"I called on *Tiferet* when you were knocked out. I saw you and Eli," Nykima said. "Then I heard a static before your body woke up without you."

"It... it was Cora," Leah said.

"The high priestess?" Nykima asked.

"I think so. It sounded like her, but Eli said she's dead."

Sarah stepped forward, folding her arms. "Why do you care?"

Nykima's eyes widened. "Because I saw how shaken up Eli was. Something that gets to him that way must be huge."

"But he thinks it's a trap," Isaac said.

Nykima shook her head. "He knows it could be something, but he knows the Infinity Board won't act on it. He knows you three won't stop if you think no one's on your side. Luckily, I don't need to abide by Board rules anymore."

The door swung open behind Leah, and Madeline glided in wearing a bright white dress. "Nykima, thank you for escorting these Mystics." Madeline looked at Leah and her friends. "Please, come. We have much to discuss."

As they were led into a circular chamber lit only by flickering candles, Leah's sense of unease grew. Shadows danced across the walls, creating shifting patterns. In the center of the room stood a small table surrounded by chairs.

"Sit," Madeline instructed, gesturing to the table.

Leah hesitated, but she had nowhere else to go. She sank into a chair with a deep breath, Sarah and Isaac flanking her.

Madeline settled across from them, Nykima positioning her wheelchair nearby. The Voodoo Queen's eyes glowed in the candlelight as she studied Leah.

"You made quite the scene at the boxing gym." Madeline smiled. "I wanted to thank you personally."

Leah blinked. "Thank me?"

"Mark always had a soft spot for the 1891 faction. But now, I know exactly where his loyalties lie." Madeline leaned forward and whispered. "Plus, the 1891 poured a lot of money into those bets, and their support is dwindling as we speak."

Leah scoffed. "So, you tricked the Infinity Board into thinking they needed me to lose to make the 1891 faction unstable?"

"We all play the game, dear," Madeline said. "Just depends on how many moves ahead you are."

"And you ordered me here to what? Make the Board think the encampment was in danger?" Leah asked.

"Yes and no. Never leave your pieces in harm's way when your opponent loses money. The 1891s need to cool off, and it's best if they don't see you for now. Besides, I heard you'd connected to a voice, yes?"

Leah glanced at Nykima, then nodded. "I believe it was Cora, the High Priestess of the Immortal Witches."

"Yes, of course," Madeline stood, turning to a wall filled with jars. "Best to make the preparations, then."

"Preparations? For what?" Leah asked.

Madeline reached into a glass terrarium, pulling out two bright yellow snakes that coiled around both her arms. Their eyes glowed with an eerie yellow light that matched Madeline's gaze.

"There is a ritual we can perform," Madeline said, petting the top of one snake's head. "One that bridges the connection between you and Cora."

CHAPTER 21

CLARITY

Leah's heart raced as her eyes shifted between the smile on Madeline's face and the snakes coiled around her arms. Herbs and incense filled the room, making Leah's eyes heavy.

"I don't know about this," Sarah muttered. She shifted her weight from foot to foot, eyes fixed on the yellow snake that seemed to watch them with unnerving intelligence.

Isaac cleared his throat, looking down at the markings on the floor. "We need to be ready. In case it isn't Cora, I mean."

"Wait," Leah said, looking up at Madeline. "They're not coming with me, right?"

Madeline frowned. "Why else would I invite them? Nykima, as well. Best to have a group in case things get out of hand."

"But it's dangerous," Leah said.

"We know," Sarah said. "But this is our fight, too. You can't do everything by yourself."

Leah's throat tightened, and she shifted her feet.

Madeline smiled, her gold teeth glinting in the candle-light. "So, it's settled then. Nykima will bring you three back when the time is right. Stay close to her, understood?"

Leah looked at Nykima. After the last time she'd seen her at Le Syndicat, slumped over her vodka at that lonely corner table and lashing out about being labeled a spy and traitor by both sides, she wasn't sure if she could trust her actually to bring them back. But, in the way she sat now, back straight, and a semblance of who she was when she was a White Knight, maybe Leah could. Besides, what was the alternative?

She nodded, and Madeline turned, gesturing for them to follow. "This way."

Madeline opened a hidden door in the wall, stepping through and urging the others to follow.

Inside was a small, circular room. More candles surrounded a circle made of red powder and herbs. A weathered table stood to the side, holding what Leah recognized as the black tome she'd given them all those months ago, along with several jars.

At the snap of Madeline's fingers, they all lit, brightening the room.

A small table bearing a black book and several jars stood to the side. Madeline picked up a bit of chalk and drew circles and shapes in the ritual circle.

"Is this the same ritual we did to find Asmodeus?" Leah asked, eyeing a jar Nykima was busy filling with herbs.

Madeline filled a ceramic bowl with oil, dumping the herbs in once Nykima handed them over. A foul smell permeated the room, forcing Leah to hold back a gag.

"No," Madeline replied. "We can't track without something of theirs. This is to form a bridge between essences, which is harder, but if you can hear her call, then she should hear yours."

Isaac eyed the table. "Wait, is that the black tome?"

"It is," Nykima said, "Good eye, Bishop. Now, lay on the circle."

Madeline set the bowl on the table and opened the tome, quickly flipping through pages. The yellow snake crawled around her neck and fixed its gaze on Isaac.

"The oils are ready," Madeline announced, her tone businesslike. "We must hurry before the turn sour."

Leah lowered herself onto the cold floor, positioning herself in the circle's center. Sarah and Isaac flanked her, lying by her side.

Nykima parked her wheelchair close and dragged herself into the circle beside Isaac. "Leah, you need to picture that static voice and Cora with your mind as much as possible. We all depend on you to get there."

Madeline removed her sandals and stood with her feet on either side of Leah's head. She hummed an oddly relaxing melody that vibrated through Leah. As Madeline poured thick, warm oils around their heads, Leah fought to focus on Cora, on the static-filled voice.

The oils dripped onto Leah's forehead and into her hair; the smell was overwhelming. She felt Sarah's grip tighten and heard Isaac's sharp intake of breath. The room started spinning slowly, reminding her of her first time drinking back in high school.

Leah opened her eyes, immediately regretting it as she saw Madeline standing over them, arms extended, sharp knives glinting in each hand. The two snakes slithered down her arms, their heads hovering over Leah's belly. As Madeline's humming grew louder, the snakes coiled around each other, forming a strange knot.

Heart pounding, Leah squeezed her eyes shut as the snakes willingly slid their bodies against the knife blades. A thick, warm liquid dripped onto her. The floor gave way, and she was falling.

The strong herby scents vanished, and Leah floated in a dark void.

A distant hum disrupted the quiet, bringing Leah's awareness back. She felt hands holding her. Her friends, yet she couldn't see them. A flicker of memory surfaced—purple eyes, a static-filled voice.

"Cora," Leah whispered.

Something jerked her violently, reeling her in at dizzying speed. Leah felt the hands slipping from her grasp and tightened her grip, determined not to lose her friends in this strange place.

She sat up abruptly, scanning her own body for the gore and viscera from the snakes.

"Holy shit, that was trippy," Sarah's voice came from beside her, sounding as disoriented as Leah felt.

Nykima stood in front of them, arms folded.

"Wait, how are you standing?" Sarah asked.

Nykima pursed her lips. "We're astral projecting."

Leah looked up, recognition dawning as she took in the surroundings. The bright shop's walls covered in Americana art and tattoo designs were familiar. But it was different now, with decaying walls, peeling paint, and flickering fluorescent lights casting shadows on heavy black curtains that covered what Leah remembered as once-bright windows.

"It is good to see you, Leah."

Leah turned, following the woman's voice standing by the back door.

Cora.

The towering woman commanded attention effortlessly, but even so, Leah saw that something was off. The High Priestess seemed diminished somehow, her usual aura of power muted.

Leah scrambled to her feet. "Cora, it's good to see you,

too."

Cora's dark eyes swept over the group. "I see you brought company. Good. We don't have much time, and we'll need all the help we can get."

Sarah and Isaac moved closer to Leah. Leah could feel their unease, mirroring her growing sense of wrongness about this place.

"The Infinity Board said you were dead." Leah struggled to keep her voice steady. "They said the tattoo parlor wasn't safe. What happened? Where are we?"

Cora's expression darkened, her long locs swaying as she shook her head. "Legion attacked us shortly after you and your Queen left. We were in the middle of an initiation, and he brought an army down on us. We let our guard down for a second, giving him just enough time to strike."

Cora walked past them, stopping in front of a window with drawn curtains. "The only one he didn't get was Frank. That lucky witch gift of his let him slip through the cracks. But the rest of us are gone."

"Wait," Leah said, moving closer to Cora. "Are you saying you're dead? But you don't look like a ghost. How—"

A laugh escaped Cora's lips. "Killing the High Priestess is simple. I would be dead, but..."

She grasped the curtains and flung them open. Leah focused on the view beyond the cracked glass. A roiling mass of jet-black fog surrounded them, moving with unnatural speed. In the distance, a small, dimmed sphere hung like a dying, marbled sun streaked in black.

Cora leaned forward and whispered, "We are inside Legion."

CHAPTER 22

THE WITCHES' FATE

The void beyond the tattoo parlor's windows writhed in darkness. Leah pressed closer to Sarah and Isaac. Even Nykima, usually so composed, couldn't hide her shiver.

No, no, no, Asmodeus pleaded in Leah's mind. *Not again. We shouldn't be here.*

"There were only a few of us left alive when it happened," Cora said. Her voice carried the weight of defeat, something Leah had never expected to hear from the High Priestess. "Legion opened his mouth and drew us in. I knew we couldn't escape, so I made a choice."

The window glass crackled, another crack spider-webbing across its surface. Cora raised her hand, purple light flaring from her eyes, and the crack sealed itself. But Leah noticed how the effort made the High Priestess's hand tremble.

"You're keeping this place together," Leah realized. "All by yourself?"

Cora nodded, her eyes dimming. "What remains of it, at least. The others, their essences, help me, too. I've managed to preserve this small pocket, but it's a constant battle."

"Do you know how long you've been here?" Sarah asked, eying the cracked walls.

"Time loses meaning," Cora replied. "But based on what I've found in Legion's memories, it's been months."

Isaac took a hesitant step forward. "How did he best the Immortal Witches? Aren't you supposed to—"

"Because Legion isn't just a demon," Cora interrupted, glaring at Isaac. "I've learned he is something more. Come, I'll show you."

She led them to a window on the far side of the parlor. As they approached, Leah felt an unease build in her stomach. The glass here was clouded as if covered in a thin layer of frost. Cora placed her hand against it, and the fog cleared.

Beyond the window lay a swirling vortex of darkness, like the heart of a storm. But a pulsing sphere of light hung at its center, barely visible through the chaos. It was marbled with streaks of inky blackness that writhed and shifted as if trying to consume the light from within.

Leah narrowed her eyes. "What is that?"

Is that? A core? Asmodeus's voice resonated with a mix of awe and fear.

"A core?" Leah responded aloud, drawing curious glances from her friends.

There are legends in my realm of things that exist beyond our comprehension—creatures of pure energy. When we were at the peak of our power, some demons spoke of finding more.

Cora raised an eyebrow. "Your demon friend is right. That is an ethereal core. It's how Legion survived the Mandrake potion."

A tendril of darkness from the core lashed out from the swirling vortex, slamming against the window. Leah flinched, but the barrier held.

"It's best not to stare for long," Cora said, waving her hand and frosting the window.

She led them deeper into the parlor, past rows of empty tattoo stations, and to a door with a sign marked "PRIVATE." Cora ushered them inside and closed the door behind them. The office inside was pristine, unmarred by the decay and destruction in the parlor. Bookshelves lined the walls, and a large wooden desk dominated the center of the room. But what caught Leah's attention was the tube television perched on a filing cabinet, its curved screen and bulky antenna a relic from the 90s.

Cora approached it, her fingers hovering over the power button. "Brace yourselves. What you are about to see isn't pleasant."

The screen flickered to life, filled with static at first. Then, slowly, images began to form. The scene was chaotic and disorienting - fragments of memories flashing by in rapid succession. Faces of Mystics, both familiar and unknown, being torn apart. The attack on HQ played out from a different angle as if the viewer towered above the carnage. Glimpses of rituals and sacrifices followed, the gore making Leah's stomach churn.

"This is Legion's memories," she breathed, recognizing the distinctive purple tinge to the vision and the way the perspective shifted unnaturally, just as it had during their encounters. Fractures formed on the screen, and the images grew stranger and more broken, reflecting the fractured psyche behind them.

"The Mandrake potion did more than weaken him," Cora explained. "It destabilized the balance, nearly destroying his demon and human sides."

"Sides?" Sarah furrowed her brow. "I thought he was just a demon."

Cora shook her head. "Legion possessed Reginald. If it were that easy, then the potion would have killed Legion. But he is something more. That core gives him power beyond what any demon should possess. And that kept him alive."

Leah's mind raced, trying to process this new information. "So, can he be killed?"

"If you disrupted the balance," Isaac said, his eyes wide with realization. "Then he's hiding to stabilize himself. Meaning he *thinks* he can be killed."

Cora nodded. "Exactly. But he's running out of time. The longer he remains unstable, the more erratic and dangerous he becomes. I don't know what will happen next if we don't stop him soon."

Leah could see it playing out on the television screen—flashes of destruction, entire cities consumed by darkness.

"There has to be a way." Leah put her hand on her chin. "We need to find him and exploit this weakness."

Cora shook her head. "You need information on the core, but getting that..." She trailed off, eyeing the television. "It would be an enormous risk."

"What kind of risk?" Nykima asked.

"The information doesn't exist in our world," Cora said. "Knowledge of things like ethereal cores is scarce. There are things that see to it that information like that is kept hidden and removed from our world. But there is one place within reach that might have something."

"Where?" Leah asked.

Cora hesitated. "The Library of Alexandria."

Isaac scratched his head. "You mean the Library of Alexandria that burned?"

Cora waved him off. "That was just a copy after Alexander dreamt of the real one. "The real library has been around as long as the Trees themselves. It's the collective memory of everything the Trees created, destroyed, and touched."

"If that's the case, why hasn't the Infinity Board gone there already?" Sarah asked.

"My kind keep the coordinates hidden. We don't want a poor mortal to stumble there and lose their mind. But I trust you will keep your wits about you. If we're doing this, we need to do it now."

"What's the catch?" Nykima asked, crossing her arms. "There's *always* a catch."

Cora nodded. "There price changes, and that will be up to the Librarian to decide."

"And, what, you can't tell us any more?" Nykima asked.

Cora frowned, choosing her words carefully, "There are things in these realms that hold secrets and power far greater than you can't possibly imagine. And those things go to great lengths to ensure their deals are not spoken of."

"That sounds oddly convenient," Nykima said, not backing down.

"It is. For them." Cora took a step forward, the two faces now inches away, her voice slightly louder and more menacing than before. "I'm an immortal being that belongs to the Astral Plane. The Librarian will treat mortals differently." She paused and tilted her head. "Besides, I don't think we have another choice unless you want to keep biding your time until Legion takes the entire Board down."

"Are you coming with us?" Leah asked.

"I do that, and this place crumbles along your portal back home."

After a long silence, with the two women staring each other down, Leah spoke. "Are we doing this or what?"

Nykima glared at Cora momentarily, then dropped her gaze and stepped back. Cora nodded and walked past them to a spot near the door. She traced her hand in the air, violet light trailing behind her fingers. When she drew a circle, the center filled with light, and Cora stepped back.

"I'll keep this open for as long as possible, but hurry. Time is different in the Astral, so do your best to be in and out."

CHAPTER 23

THE LIBRARIAN

Leah was the first to step through, feeling the sensation of walking through cold water before she stood on the other with an energy in the air that made her skin prickle. She blinked, adjusting to the sudden shift in light and temperature.

"Holy shit," Sarah breathed beside her.

Leah couldn't have said it better herself. They stood at the edge of an impossible garden, a perfect square divided into four distinct sections. To her left, cherry blossoms bloomed in a sea of pink, their delicate petals drifting as if on a warm spring breeze. Directly ahead, lush green grass swayed beneath a blazing summer sun. To her right, trees blazed with autumn colors—reds and golds so vivid they almost hurt to look at. Behind them, snow covered the ground, and icicles hung on branches.

"Woah, it's beautiful," Isaac said.

Nykima reached out to touch a branch before pulling her hand away. "Don't let your guard down."

Leah nodded. The garden was mesmerizing, but it felt off. It was as if the gardens were stitched together from different gardens in different worlds.

"Come on." Nykima gestured towards a path that led through the garden's center. "In and out, remember?"

As they walked, Leah felt her temperature fluctuate wildly. One moment, she was hot and sweating in the summer heat; the next, she shivered and her breath fogged. The shifts were nauseating.

"Anyone else feeling like they're gonna throw up?" Sarah asked, holding her stomach.

"It's like having a hangover," Isaac agreed.

They rounded a bend in the gardens, and the trees cleared. The Library of Alexandria stood looming before them.

The building seemed to defy the laws of physics with its impossible angles stretching into a star-filled void where a sky should have been. White marble gleamed with an inner light that hurt Leah's eyes if she looked at it too long.

As they approached the towering entrance, Leah noted intricate carvings covering every surface. Ancient symbols and elaborate scenes shifted and changed as she watched as if they were living.

"Look." Isaac pointed to a section near the base of a column. "That looks like the fall of Rome... and now it's changing to the Renaissance."

Sarah leaned in closer, squinting at the carvings. "Is that... us? At headquarters?"

Leah followed Sarah's gaze and found familiar faces etched into the stone. Portraits of herself, Sarah, Isaac, and even Gabe stared back at her. The scene played out in excruciatingly accurate detail right up until Legion attacked. Then, it shifted, becoming something else entirely.

"This place knows everything," Nykima said, her fingers brushing against the stone. "We could learn so much from these stones alone."

Leah pulled herself away from the shifting stone. She could spend hours there, watching history and the future unfold, losing herself. She shivered at the thought and focused on the massive doors before them.

That's when she noticed the inscription carved above the entrance. The symbols were like nothing she'd ever seen, twisting and writhing as if alive. As she watched, they rearranged themselves, forming words she could read:

Time sows the seeds of Knowledge, from which the roots of Wisdom sprout. Wisdom then branches into Insight, and from Insight blossoms Patience. With Patience, the fruits of Time ripen, sowing seeds anew. But fruits plucked before their season turn bitter, and their seeds yield poisoned trees.

"Well, that's not ominous," Leah muttered.

Before she could dwell on it further, the doors swung open with a sound like a thunderclap.

Darkness loomed inside, and for a moment, no one moved.

"We've come this far," Leah said, looking back at her friends. "No turning back now." She took a deep breath and stepped inside.

As her eyes adjusted, she spotted tiny flames floating in mid-air, illuminating shelf after endless shelf of books.

The library stretched forever, with marbled staircases spiraling into the void, twisting and intersecting at strange angles. Books filled every corner of the space, making up the walls and piled on the stairs. It was more books than Leah could have imagined existing in all the world.

"This is incredible," Isaac said, walking toward the nearest shelf.

"Keep an eye out," Nykima said, her eyes glowing yellow. "I don't like the looks of this place."

Sarah whistled low. "How the hell are we supposed to find anything in here?"

"I believe I can be of assistance with that."

The voice resonated from every direction, forcing Leah to freeze. She whirled around, searching for the source, and found herself face-to-face with a strange figure.

It towered over them, a mass of tattered robes and a pale white face with a massive sharp-fanged mouth and a face covered in eyes of every color, some human, some animal, and others glowing. As Leah stepped back, arm after arm extended out from the robes, far too many for one being to have, each running a finger along the shelves, grabbing books and replacing them with others from under its robes.

"Welcome, seekers of knowledge," the being said, its voice a collection of whispers. "I am the Librarian."

This thing, Asmodeus whispered, his voice strained. *Leah, you must run. It's not safe, and this thing can tear you apart in seconds. We have to—*

"We've come seeking information on Legion," Leah said, standing her ground.

The Librarian's many eyes blinked in unison, a sight that made Leah's stomach churn. "Ah yes, the devourer. An interesting subject matter."

It glided closer to Leah, inspecting her. Leah fought every urge to back away.

"You will find that information here," it continued, "but as with all things here, there is a price to be paid."

"What kind of price?" Isaac asked from behind Leah

The Librarian's form rippled, and Leah could have sworn she saw the ghost of a smile. "Memories," it said. "A fair exchange, wouldn't you agree? Knowledge for knowledge."

Leah frowned. "*Our* memories?"

"Yes. One from each of you." The Librarian's arms

continued pulling and reshelving books. "A small price to pay for secrets, wouldn't you say?"

Nykima's eyes narrowed. "How does that work? And if we agree, how will we know that you'll give us what we need without making us give more?"

The Librarian's many arms gestured expansively. "I am bound by the laws of this place, just as the laws of your world bind you. I cannot lie nor take back a bargain struck."

Leah's mind raced. The thought of losing even a single memory was terrifying, but what choice did they have? Legion was out there, growing stronger by the day. If they didn't find a way to stop him soon, then what?

"We'll do it," she said, her voice coming on stronger than she felt.

"Leah, wait," Isaac started, but she glared at him.

"We need this information," she said. "Whatever it costs, it's worth saving everyone we have left."

Sarah nodded. "I'm in."

"As am I," Nykima added.

Isaac hesitated a moment longer, then sighed. "Fine. Let's do this."

The Librarian slipped all their hands beneath their robes, standing tall before Leah. "Very well. Form a circle and grab hands."

Leah did as she was told, and the others followed suit, forming a circle around the Librarian. The Librarian's many arms stretched towards them, cold fingers pressing against Leah's forehead.

No! Asmodeus's voice thundered in her mind. *I won't be a part of this.*

"You have to," Leah whispered. "You want to defeat Legion, right?"

For a moment, she thought he might refuse. Then she

felt his resistance crumble like a wall giving way, his essence softening within her mind.

Fine, Asmodeus said.

The Librarian's touch sent a jolt through Leah's body. The world around her faded, replaced by a whirlwind of images and sensations. Her entire life flashed before her eyes in a dizzying blur.

She saw herself as a child, laughing as her father pushed her on a swing. She relived her first day at the Academy, the nervousness and excitement. She felt the warmth of Gabe's embrace, the ache of loss when he was gone.

The memories came faster and faster, and her life compressed into mere seconds. Leah's head throbbed, her vision swimming as she struggled to hold onto something. She wasn't sure what, but she knew it was important.

Then, abruptly, her mind cleared.

Leah gasped, her eyes flying open. She was back in the library, surrounded by her friends. They all wore similar expressions of disorientation and loss.

"It is done," the Librarian intoned.

Leah blinked, trying to clear the fog from her mind. There was a void, a blank space where something should have been.

"What did you take?" she asked.

The Librarian smiled wide, baring their fangs. "That which was given. You need not concern yourself with it now."

Leah wanted to argue and demand answers, but she knew she wouldn't get anything from this thing. She looked at her friends, seeing her confusion mirrored in their faces.

"Now," the Librarian said, its many arms gesturing towards a section of shelves that hadn't been there a moment before. "Let me show you what you came here to learn."

"Show you?" Leah asked.

The Librarian smiled, reaching four long, pale hands forward and tapping each of their temples. "Close your eyes and remember."

The world fell away, and Leah found herself plunged into memory.

CHAPTER 24

TOUGH MEMORIES

Leah crouched in a dimly lit tiled room that reeked of scotch and blood. Her heart pounded as she peered around the corner, drawn by a sound she couldn't quite place.

What she saw made her stomach turn in knots.

An old man lay naked on the floor, surrounded by symbols drawn in blood. As Leah watched, the man's body jerked upward, suspended in midair by invisible strings.

A low, raspy voice filled the room. "I won't let you go that easily. Her spells can't stop me. You are mine, and you had one job."

The older man's body contorted unnaturally. His spine twisted as several ribs snapped, jutting through his skin like broken branches. His limbs bent backward at the joints, bones splintering with wet, sickening cracks. Blood sprayed from fresh wounds, splattering across the symbols on the floor.

"And you failed," the voice growled.

Leah wanted to run, to scream, to do anything but watch this grotesque scene again. But she couldn't move, her eyes unable to tear away.

As quickly as it began, the memory faded. Leah gasped, her eyes flying open as she found herself back in the Library. The Librarian's cold touch lingered on her temple.

"Interesting," they mused. "There is more to uncover. Let us delve deeper."

Before Leah could protest, she was pulled into another memory.

This time, she stood in a dark corridor, facing a large metal door. Two unconscious Black Knights lay at her feet. With a metallic groan, the door swung open, revealing a battered and bloodied Ian Kim tied to a chair.

Ian's head jerked up, his eyes wild with fear and desperation. "But I did everything you asked," he pleaded. "You promised we'd change the world. You promised I'd see the day it all changed. I did what you wanted, didn't I? Please—"

A shadowy figure waved dismissively, cutting off Ian's desperate words. Its voice was distorted when it spoke, rising and falling in an unnatural cadence.

"Just get it over with. I don't have all night."

Leah blinked, and suddenly, she was pinned against the wall, a clawed hand wrapped around her throat. The shadowy figure loomed over her, its features indistinct.

"You've become quite the nuisance, Leah Ackerman," it hissed, its voice a cacophony whispers. "Always poking your head around."

The grip on her throat tightened, cutting off her air. Leah struggled, her vision darkening. Just as she thought she might pass out, the scene shifted again.

Now she stood in a darkened room, shadows stretching across the floor and up heavy wool curtains. Flakes of ash drifted through the air like snowflakes, settling on a massive mahogany desk. Behind it sat a high-backed leather chair facing away from Leah toward a roaring stone fireplace.

A soft, melodic, and strangely familiar voice drifted from behind the chair. "There is only a handful outside our grasp. I doubt they'll even be a threat."

The gravelly voice that responded was even more familiar now, his voice echoing from every corner of the room at once.

"They need to be dealt with," Legion growled. "I won't have us taking any chances."

Leah's heart raced as she tried to peer around the chair, desperate to glimpse who Legion was speaking to. But the shadows clung to the figure unnaturally, forming a blackened silhouette that rested its head in its hands.

"Very well," the shadow figure replied, its long fingers wrapping around the arms of the chair. "But there isn't much I can do. The ritual keeps their locations secret for a reason."

"Leave that to me," Legion said. "I have the right candidate. Remember Asmodeus? Who was it that defeated him?"

The memory dissolved, and Leah was back in the Library, gasping for breath.

Sarah's legs gave out, and she sank to the floor. "I saw them all die again," she choked out. "The Queen's Gambit... everyone."

Isaac knelt beside Sarah, wrapping an arm around her shoulders. "There was so much blood."

That was bloody awful.

"What did you see?" Leah asked Asmodeus.

I relieved my fight with Legion for the Kyjak title. The moment he defeated me.

Nykima glared at the Librarian as she stood tall. "I didn't need to relive that."

The Librarian stepped back, eyes trained on Leah, unblinking. "All of your experiences have been so illuminating. I know precisely what it is you need."

The Librarian turned, walking down an aisle of books, waving the group on as multiple hands grabbed books and hid them beneath the creature's robes.

They followed for a long while, trailing through shelves and climbing stairs. Every so often, they would pass by someone with a stack of books beside them, their forms emaciated and their hands trembling as they weakly turned pages, muttering to themselves.

Finally, they stopped at a table, and the Librarian placed several tattered books, scrolls, and, oddly, a laptop on it. "The knowledge you seek is here. His origins, his strengths, and any recorded weaknesses. They are placed in chronological order. Summon me if you have any questions."

And with that, the Librarian trailed off into the nearby stacks, leaving the four of them in the middle of the missive library.

CHAPTER 25

THE LEGEND BEHIND THE MONSTER

"Well," Sarah said as she drummed her fingers on the table. "this isn't creepy at all."

Leah nodded, looking down at the ancient scrolls and laptops scattered across the polished wood. "Well, let's get started." She reached for the nearest scroll.

As her fingers brushed the parchment, the strange symbols etched upon it began to writhe and squirm, rearranging into familiar English letters. Leah jerked her hand back with a gasp.

"Did you see that?" she asked, looking up at the others.

Isaac leaned in with wide eyes. "Fascinating. It's like the arch above the doorway. Maybe everything here automatically translates."

Nykima flipped open a book, gently flipping the pages. "Be wary. We don't know what kind of magic this is; all magic comes with a price. Let's hope those memories were all it takes."

Leah nodded and unrolled the scroll fully. The others gathered around, their shoulders pressed close as they began to read.

"Chief Kal," Leah read aloud, her voice barely above a

whisper. "We are surrounded and desperate. As suspected, the Rus have mastered the rituals to harness the demons, their power growing immensely. We've learned they are experimenting with a scroll, trying to summon something beyond the demons..."

As she continued reading, Leah felt Asmodeus stir within her. She could feel him reading the words with her, fascinated by its contents.

A scroll? he murmured in her mind. *That could be the beginning of Legion.*

Leah set the letter down, looking at the massive pile before them. "This is going to take forever." She picked up a small book. "We need to just keep going. Shout out if you find anything."

Leah unrolled another ancient scroll, the parchment crackling beneath her touch. Around her, Nykima, Sarah, and Isaac hunched over their own texts. The shelves seemed to lean inward, as if listening. More than once, Leah caught movement in the corners of her vision, only to find nothing but shadows when she looked.

The story they started piecing together was haunting. The letters showed a tribe fighting against an army of demon-possessed warriors. Their words grew more frantic with each letter, filling with more and more ink splatters and shaky handwriting. And through it all, mentions of a scroll that promised salvation—their last, desperate hope against annihilation. It was a ritual designed to create a being of immense power. And at the center of it all, a warrior named Nis.

"This Nis guy," Sarah said, tossing down another letter. "He's Legion, isn't he?"

Leah nodded. "It has to be. Listen to this..." She read from another scroll detailing Nis's transformation. "Unity.

That's what Nis is preaching. His power surpasses that of a legion of Demon Warriors."

"A Legion," Isaac repeated, his face pale. "That's not subtle."

Asmodeus's voice rumbled in Leah's mind. *There were legends in my realm. Stories of our people being abducted. Some came back talking about beings beyond our comprehension.*

"But if that's true," Nykima said slowly after Leah relayed the information, "then what exactly are we dealing with? What is Legion? What is this ethereal core?"

Before anyone could answer, Isaac held up another scroll. "You need to hear this," he said, his voice cracking. "It's about Nis. He's talking about an uncontrollable hunger and turning into something monstrous."

Leah nodded. "That's Legion, then."

"There's more," Isaac said, his eyes scanning further down the letter. "Something about a ritual to extract an ethereal core. But..." He frowned, flipping the scroll over. "It cuts off. The rest of the information isn't here."

Leah took the letter from Isaac and then flipped through several books. "That ritual, help me find it."

They spent several minutes in silence, everyone pilfering through the contents. Still, no one came up with any further mention of this ritual.

"Wait a second," Isaac said suddenly, his brow furrowed. "The Librarian said we'd find *most* of the information here. They emphasized the word 'most' when they said it."

Leah tilted her head, recalling what the Librarian said. "So, you think they are hiding more?"

Isaac nodded, then called out, his voice echoing in the vast space. "Librarian! We need you!"

For a moment, nothing happened. Then, Leah heard a rush of air and the sound of many legs thudding on the ground. The Librarian emerged from the shelves, their many eyes blinking in unsettling unison as they regarded them.

"You have a question?" they asked.

"The ritual scroll," Isaac said, gesturing to the letter. "Why isn't that in this?"

The Librarian's lip twitched in a quick smile. "Perceptive," it murmured. "Yes, the information in my possession is incomplete."

"Incomplete?" Leah echoed. "But I thought this place was supposed to hold all knowledge."

All the Librarian's eyes focused on Leah. "All knowledge that exists within the realms I oversee resides in these walls. Unless those things are taken and stored beyond my reach."

"Taken?" Sarah asked. "By who?"

The Librarian meandered to the table, picking up several books and opening the pages. "The scroll you seek was stolen," they finally said. "Years ago, by two individuals wishing to destroy a foe." Their eyes lingered on Leah, their lips stretching in a wide smile.

"Who?" she asked. "Who stole it?"

"They went by the names Helen Nielsen," the Librarian paused, tilting their head, "and Elizabeth Mizrahi."

CHAPTER 26

THE THIEF'S DAUGHTER

The Librarian's many eyes fixed upon Leah, her heart pounding as each one blinked in unsettling unison.

"My mom?" Leah asked. "Wait, but how?"

The creature's form seemed to ripple and shift, growing larger until it towered over Leah. "The thief that is your mother came seeking power to fend off an entire legion of demons. And she stole the very knowledge she sought."

Sarah stepped closer to Leah, siding up to her in silent support. Nykima crossed her arms, ready to say something when Isaac spoke first.

"But that doesn't make any sense," Isaac said. "If that's true, then you're suggesting what, that Leah's mom summoned Legion?"

"You all seek the truth about Legion's origins, yes?" the Librarian intoned. "Are you prepared for what that truth may reveal about those closest to you?"

If this thing can take memories, then perhaps they can also show them, Asmodeus said.

Leah nodded and looked the Librarian in their many eyes. "Can you show us what happened?"

The Librarian grinned as many hands stretched out from under their robes and grabbed onto all four of them. Suddenly, the library around them blurred and shifted. Colors bled together, reforming into the library's entrance. But it looked off from the entrance they had come through.

Leah felt Sarah and Isaac's presence beside her, their shoulders pressed close as the world transformed. Nykima's sharp intake of breath echoed their collective awe as the past unfolded before them.

Two figures dressed in matching maroon uniforms stepped through the massive doorway, and Leah's breath caught in her throat. One was unmistakably Helen—younger but with the same pale blond hair and piercing blue eyes. And beside her...

"Mom," Leah whispered, her voice cracking.

Elizabeth Mizrahi looked so much like Leah, with the same long brown hair tied back in a ponytail and the same amber eyes. But there was a weariness to her that Leah had never seen in photos, a haunted look that Leah was all too familiar with.

"They sought power beyond mortal comprehension," the Librarian narrated as the scene unfolded. "Power to vanquish a great evil they called Asmodeus."

Leah felt a jolt at the name. She knew they'd face Asmodeus somewhere deep inside, but hearing it spoken aloud—knowing he now resided within her—made it hit harder.

She steeled herself and watched, transfixed, as her mother and Helen approached a past version of the Librarian. They both submitted to the Librarian's touch, remaining still as its many hands pulled out two books and frantically wrote in silvery ink.

"Their request was too vast," the present-day Librarian commented, waving their hands and transforming the space around them into a small table within the library. "So I guided them to begin here."

Time blurred forward as Leah watched her mother and Helen pore through scrolls and books, the Librarian constantly bringing new texts and taking others away. Leah couldn't say how much time had passed, but her mother and Helen grew gaunt, dark circles deepening beneath their eyes.

What happened to them?" Leah asked.

"This place," Sarah muttered. "Look at what it did to them."

Isaac nodded. "How long have we been here? "

"Time moves differently here, yes? How much time do we have left here?" Nykima asked the Librarian.

"The library isn't designed for mortals." The Librarian rolled its many eyes. "You are all so finite."

Leah looked back at her friends and noticed that they, too, had bags under their eyes and looser clothes. How long had they been there? It felt like only a few hours, yet they'd read through all those books and scrolls.

Time slowed, and Helen and Elizabeth hovered over a letter, calling for the Librarian.

"Yes?" the memory version of the Librarian asked, appearing from behind the stacks.

"This letter from Chief Kal," Helen said. "It speaks of a ritual scroll. And they keep using the word ethereal. Are these tied? Do you have an ethereal scroll?"

"Ah, and you think this is the answer to your question?" the Librarian asked. "You wish to summon beings from the far reaches of reality? This is the power you ask for?"

"Yes," Elizabeth answered.

The Librarian pulled an old scroll from within their robes, sealed it with a silvery wax, and handed it over.

Leah and the others moved closer as Helen and Elizabeth broke the seal and rolled out the scroll on the table. Drawings of chains bordered the parchment, and strange sigils of intersecting lines and triangles. At the center of the scroll was an oval with the outline of a hand and a word that translated into ethereal.

"This is it," Helen said, her voice tinged with awe. "We could stop Asmodeus with this. We could stop all of them."

The scene blurred again, and they were back at the library entrance. Helen and Elizabeth faced the past Librarian, the scroll clutched tightly in Elizabeth's hands.

"You may not remove that from these halls," the past Librarian intoned, dozens of hands pointing at the scroll.

"We need it," Elizabeth said. "The ritual requires this scroll to use it. If we don't, people will die."

"Knowledge may not leave these grounds. I strongly advise against further attempts, lest you wish all your memories to be lost."

Elizabeth shook her head and looked back at Helen. In one swift motion, Helen pulled out a piece of paper and incinerated it in a burst of light. Seconds late, a violet portal opened.

The past Librarian rushed forward, but Helen and Elizabeth slipped through the portal, and it closed before they reached them.

The vision faded, and Leah and her friends were back at the table.

"So, that's how they did it," Sarah muttered, breaking the silence. "They had help from an Immortal Witch."

The Librarian nodded. "That was the last time I saw that scroll."

Isaac nodded, his brow furrowed in concentration. "Why didn't you go after it?"

"Because I cannot leave the library."

"But what does the scroll do?" Nykima cut in. "Cora

said Legion is a demon and this ethereal thing inside a person. So what? If those letters were right, those warriors used demons for power but wanted more. Does this scroll call a demon god or something?"

The Librarian let out a small laugh but remained otherwise silent.

Leah shook her head. "We won't know until we talk to Queen Helen."

Isaac nodded. "They used the scroll to kill Asmodeus, but it somehow brought Legion here or gave him power. Either way, I haven't heard of this scroll until today, which means Helen has been hiding that information from everyone or all the Queens have."

"What if the ritual went wrong?" Leah asked. "Sure, they got Asmodeus in the end, but what if they didn't know?"

The Librarian's many eyes fixed on Leah. "That kind of magic was never meant for mortal hands. If wielded improperly, then entire worlds could collapse."

"If Helen still has the scroll, why hasn't she used it to defeat Legion?" Nykima asked. "If it summons him, then it should have a release too. Why hasn't she done it, or at the very least informed the infinity Board so we could be looking for the answer?"

The Librarian folded their many arms and looked at the four of them with something that Leah thought was pity. "Unfortunately, actions carry consequences."

Leah frowned. "What does that mean?"

But before she could get an answer, her body turned, Asmodeus taking control. *Run!* he shouted.

She looked over her shoulder, the Librarian moving swiftly, grabbing onto Sarah, Isaac, and Nykima before they could move.

"No," Leah strained. "We have to go back!"

Asmodeus held control, tearing through the library as a rumble sounded behind them. In no time, they made it to the entrance.

She was mere feet away from the door when the Librarian landed in front of it, slowly stepping toward her.

"Why?" Leah asked. "Why are you doing this?"

"I'm sorry," the Librarian's voice echoed. "But debts incurred must be settled. Your mother stole knowledge from these halls. Now you, her daughter, and your friends must remain to balance the scales."

CHAPTER 27
DEAL

Leah stepped back, looking left and right for any sign of escape as she faced the Librarian. Their many eyes blinked in unsettling unison. The massive doors of the library loomed ahead, and the pounding echoed just beyond the muffled cries of her friends.

"You can't do this," Leah said, her voice steadier than she felt. "I paid the price. I had nothing to do with what my mother stole."

The Librarian stood tall, taking slow steps toward her. "Mortals carry the burdens of their ancestors. You are the daughter of a thief, and the debt must be paid."

Leah's fists clenched at her sides. She called on *Malchut*, imagining the energy pooling into her fists. But as she expected the familiar serpent to come forth, nothing came. The familiar energy was empty, no matter which well she called on.

"No," she whispered, panic clawing at her chest as she looked down at her hands. "I... why?"

The Librarian smiled. "You belong to the library now. Your access to your trees may be granted upon request. For now, I am in need of a cataloger to help catch up on thousands of years of wisdom."

"Wait," Leah said, her mind reeling. "I can't. They need—"

The Librarian gestured to the door. "They will survive. Or they won't. But by the time your debt is paid, the memory of your friends will have long since turned to dust."

"No, no, no!" Leah shook her head. "There has to be something. Some way—"

Asmodeus took over Leah's body, facing the Librarian. "What if we return the scroll to you?"

The Librarian paused, its countless eyes focusing on her with laser intensity. "Explain."

Asmodeus drew a deep breath, pausing to collect his thoughts. "Elizabeth Mizrahi is no longer with us. That leaves one person who knows of the scroll. Helen Nielsen. Would that settle the debt if we bring it back to you?"

The Librarian considered, hesitating for a moment. "My collection will be whole again. But how can I trust the words of a thief's daughter?"

Leah pushed through Asmodeus's control, regaining control of her body. "Because I'm not my mother," she shot back. "And I keep my promises."

The Librarian turned away, many fingers tapping their lips. "But to trust an unleashed hound to return home is a foolish endeavor."

"Then mark me," Leah said.

What? Leah, no, Asmodeus said. *This isn't a demon. You can't—*

"Mark you?" the Librarian asked.

"You can do that, right? Put a bit of you in me?" She held up her arm. "Demons can do it. I can't imagine you wouldn't know how to do the same."

The Librarian's eyes gleamed. "A part of me? Yes. yes, that could work." They paused for a moment, then raised an eyebrow. "You have yourself a deal. But know this, little Leah Ackerman. If you fail me, the consequences will be dire and eternal."

"Consequences? You mean worse than being stuck here cataloging?" Leah asked.

"This bargain comes threefold. You break this, and I will see to it your mind, soul, and body are mine."

Leah shivered. "How long would I have?"

"Three turnings of your rocky planet to retrieve the scroll and return it to these halls."

Three days? That should work if she moved quickly. Why would Helen need the scroll anyway? She wouldn't deny Leah if she outright asked. Would she? That is, assuming Helen still had the scroll in the first place.

This is madness, Asmodeus hissed in her mind. *Three days, or we're this thing's play toy for all eternity?*

Leah took a deep breath and stepped forward. "I accept your terms."

The Librarian smiled, reaching one pale hand up and plucking an eye free from their head. It lowered the eye, a black, inky void with a single point of light that shifted inside.

"Then let it be done," the Librarian's voice boomed.

Before Leah could react, the Librarian gripped her arm with several hands and held her palm open, placing the eye on top. She tried to stumble back, but they held her in place. The eye sank into her skin, white-hot pain searing her mind.

Leah squeezed her eyes shut, gritting her teeth against the agony. When she finally forced them open again, she saw the eye nestled in the center of her palm, its white pupil fixated on her.

"I will be watching," the Librarian said. "Every moment, every breath. Do not think to deceive me, Leah Ackerman."

The massive doors swung open, and the Librarian pushed her out. She caught herself just before falling, her legs shaky beneath her.

As the doors closed, she heard the Librarian say, "Your time starts now. Three days to retrieve the scroll, or you are mine in body, mind, and soul."

CHAPTER 28
A ROUGH RETURN

Leah stepped through the violet portal, followed by Nykima, Sarah, and Isaac. The world twisted and distorted around her and her friends. For a moment, Leah felt as if she were being torn apart, her very atoms scattered across the vastness of the Astral Plane.

Then, with a lurch, they tumbled onto the cracked floor of the tattoo parlor.

Cora stood before them, her usually regal posture now hunched with exhaustion. Her eyes widened as she took them in.

"What happened?" Cora helped Leah to her feet as the portal closed. "You look like you've been through hell."

Leah opened her mouth to respond, but the words caught in her throat.

Sarah spoke up. "There's a scroll we have to find. One that Helen stole, and we think she used to summon Legion."

Cora's face darkened. "I see," she murmured. "Did you learn anything else?"

As Isaac recounted their discoveries about Legion's origins and the ethereal core, Leah's mind raced. She needed to tell them about the bargain, about the eye now nestled in her palm. But the words refused to come, and the eye wasn't there when she looked down at her hand.

"Leah?" Cora's voice cut through her spiraling thoughts. "What aren't you telling us?"

Leah met the High Priestess's stare. She opened her mouth, ready to confess everything—

A violent tremor shook the room, forming cracks in the walls.

"We're out of time," Cora said, raising her hands above her head. "He can sense the energy in here. You four need to go. Now!"

"But—" Leah started.

"No buts," Cora cut her off. "Find Helen. Get that scroll. I'll be in contact when I can." With a wave of her hand, another shimmering portal materialized. "This will take you back to your bodies. It's been quite some time since you've been gone; let's hope whoever was on the other side was tending to you."

Leah nodded and stepped up to the portal. "Thank you, Cora. For everything."

The High Priestess smiled. "Go. And Leah?" Her gaze sharpened. "Whatever price you paid in that Library, make it worth it."

The world dissolved into a kaleidoscope of color and sensation. Leah felt as if she were falling through an endless void. Then—

Pain.

It slammed into her, every nerve ending screaming as her consciousness violently reconnected with her physical form. Leah's eyes flew open, only to wince at the harsh fluorescent light. She tried to move, but her limbs felt like lead.

"Leah? Leah, can you hear me?"

The voice sounded distant, muffled as if coming from underwater. She blinked, trying to bring the world into focus. She was lying on a cot, surrounded by medical equipment. An IV line snaked from her arm, and the steady beep of a heart monitor filled the air.

"W—where?" she croaked.

"You three need to hurry," Nykima said, her voice raspy as she held up a letter. "Get up, now!"

"What's happening?" Sarah asked as she sat up, her curly hair everywhere.

Nykima pulled the IV out of her arm and bandaged up. "We've been in the Astral for almost a week. There was an attack. You three need to go now!"

Leah stood on trembling legs, using the wall for balance. She helped Isaac and Sarah up as Nykima got into her wheelchair and guided them through the small secret door and back into the main room.

A loud, thunderous roar sounded as they entered the room. Leah froze when she spotted a huge man in the corner. His skin was grey and marred by massive gashes.

"What is that?" Isaac yelled.

"It won't hurt you," Nykima said. "Madeline put him here to protect us. You three need to go on straight to camp. Don't stop for anyone. Don't trust anyone. Just get to Helen."

Leah nodded and rushed down the hall and up the stairs. The sun was setting by the time they were on the main street.

By the time they reached camp, Leah was already exhausted. She stopped in her tracks as she caught sight of the camp.

Half the place had been burned to the ground, leaving tattered and singed tents behind. Mystics in white plastic suits moved about the place, shoveling rubble and debris.

Leah took a step forward, and her entire body froze. She could only move her eyes, and as she did, she saw one of the suited Mystics approaching with a rifle in hand while the other stood still, holding the gesture for *Hod*.

"Halt! This area is off limits!" the man shouted.

As soon as he stepped closer, his eyes grew wide. "Leah Ackerman? You're... You're alive!" He turned back and shouted. "Drop *Hod*. It's Leah Ackerman! She's back!"

Leah's body relaxed alongside Sarah and Isaac.

"Please, come on," the guard said. "We need to get you to the safe zone."

"What happened here?" Leah asked.

The guard's shoulders slumped. "The 1891 faction," he said, his voice heavy. "They struck us right after you and the others disappeared. We've been fighting them off, but..."

He trailed off, gesturing helplessly at the destruction around them.

"We need to find Queen Helen," Leah said, her voice ringing with authority she didn't entirely feel. "Now."

CHAPTER 29

CONSEQUENCES

Sarah and Isaac flanked Leah as she approached the command tent. The camp around them was in tatters, with scorched earth and smoke hanging in the air. Mystics in white hazmat suits moved through the wreckage, their faces hidden behind masks as they cleared debris.

"This is bad," Sarah muttered, looking around the ruins. "Really bad."

Isaac nodded, his face pale. "They kicked us when we were down. Why would they do that?"

Guilt churned in Leah's stomach. They'd been gone for what felt like mere hours, but the devastation around them spoke of days. As they neared the scorched Victorian home, raised voices could be heard from within.

"I don't care what excuses you have!" Jan Xie's voice cut through the air like a whip. "Find them, or I'll have your titles stripped faster than you can blink!"

Leah took a deep breath, squaring her shoulders before entering the house. Jan Xie stood in the living room with her back to them and her hands planted firmly on a makeshift war table. She whirled around at the sound of their entrance, her single eye blazing with fury.

"Where the hell have you been?" she roared, stalking towards them.

Leah opened her mouth to respond, but Jan Xie cut her off with a raised hand. "Do you have any idea what happened when you three decided to take an unauthorized field trip?"

"Black Queen, we—" Isaac began, but Jan Xie's glare silenced him.

"Half the camp is in ruins," she snarled, her voice low. "The 1891 faction saw our weakness and struck. We lost Squares, Knights, even a Rook." Her one visible eye narrowed, focusing on Leah. "And where was our hero? Madeline said she didn't have you. Said you three never showed up."

"That's a lie," Leah said. "We didn't mean to be gone so long, but we—"

"Doesn't matter," Jan Xie snapped. "What I care about is that your absence nearly cost us everything. First, you shame us with the boxing match, then this?" She shook her head. "This is beyond irresponsible."

Sarah clenched her fists at her sides as she stepped forward. "We were trying to find a way to stop Legion. If you'd just listen—"

"Enough!" Jan Xie's voice cracked. "I've had it with your insubordination. Leah Ackerman, I hereby strip you of your Black Knight title. Same for your friends. You're all demoted to—"

"You will do no such thing, Jan."

The door creaked loudly as Helen entered with a presence immediately commanding attention. Leah's eyes widened as she took in her appearance. Helen looked diminished somehow. Her skin was pale, almost ashen, and dark circles shadowed her eyes. She moved with a slight limp, one hand pressed against her side as if in pain.

Jan Xie's nostrils flared. "Helen, you can't be serious. After everything that's happened—"

"I'm quite serious," Helen interrupted, calm but firm. "To nullify someone's title, you need written approval from Micah and signatures from all the Queens. You know the rules, Jan."

A muscle twitched in Jan Xie's jaw. "The rules can be changed."

Helen's eyes flashed. "Funny, coming from you, who always favors upholding them. I didn't realize it depended on convenience."

The tension in the tent was palpable as the two Queens faced off. Leah glanced at Sarah and Isaac, seeing her own unease mirrored in their expressions.

Finally, Jan Xie broke the stare-down, turning back to Leah and her friends. "This isn't over. You three are on thin ice. One more slip-up and not even Helen can save you."

With that, she stormed out of the house, leaving behind a heavy silence.

Helen sighed as she turned to face Leah and her friends. "I'm glad to see you three are alright," she said, her voice softer now. "We were worried when you disappeared."

Leah swallowed, her throat suddenly dry. This was it—she needed to ask. Now or never.

"Helen," she began. "We need to talk. About the scroll."

Helen's expression didn't change, but Leah caught the slight tensing of her shoulders. "What scroll?"

"Don't," Leah said, surprising herself with the strength in her voice. "Please, don't lie. Not now. Not to me."

For a long moment, Helen said nothing. Then, she lowered herself into a nearby chair.

"How much do you know?"

Leah glanced at Sarah and Isaac, drawing strength from their presence. "We know you and my mother stole it from the Library of Alexandria. We know you used it to summon something. Something you thought would help you defeat Asmodeus."

Helen's eyes widened slightly. "The library? But how—"

"That's not important right now," Leah pressed on. "What matters is that scroll. Helen, we know it's connected to Legion somehow."

A flicker of something passed across Helen's face. Fear? Guilt? It was gone too quickly for Leah to be sure.

"That's... that's impossible," Helen said.

"Is it?" Isaac stepped forward. "Because from what we've learned, the timing lines up pretty well. You use this scroll to summon some great power, and not long after, Legion shows up."

Helen shook her head, but Leah could see the cracks forming in her composure. "You don't understand. The power we called upon was pure, it was unity, it was—"

"An ethereal," Leah finished.

The color drained from Helen's face. "How?"

Leah drew a deep breath, steeling herself. "Because we've seen inside Legion. Cora's alive in there. He's not just a demon, Helen. He's something more. Something with an ethereal core."

Helen's eyes closed, and her expression was one of profound weariness. When she spoke again, she could only let out a whisper.

"We never meant for any of this to happen."

"What happened?" Sarah asked. "Please, we need to know."

Helen's eyes opened, and Leah was struck by the pain she saw there. "After Asmodeus killed our former master, your mother and I wanted revenge. We'd heard whispers of a power beyond anything we'd ever encountered. Something that could rival even the mightiest demons."

"The scroll," Leah said.

Helen nodded. "We thought we could control it. Use it to destroy Asmodeus and protect humanity. But the power... it was more than we could have ever imagined. It overwhelmed us. And then—"

"It escaped," Isaac finished.

"Yes," Helen whispered. "We never saw it again. Until—"

"Until Legion appeared," Leah said, the pieces falling into place.

Helen nodded. "I didn't want to believe it at first. How could I?"

Leah's mind raced. "So, the power you summoned merged with or possessed Reginald Platt?"

"It's possible," Helen admitted. "I haven't found much about these ethereals since. So, it's hard to say what happened to it."

Sarah leaned forward. "But if that's true, then how do we stop him? He's not just a demon."

"There might be a way." Helen put her hand to her chin. "The ritual we performed left an echo. Residual energy that lingers in the place where it was cast. If we could return there, tap into that power, then we just might—"

"Use it against Legion," Leah finished, a spark of hope igniting her chest.

Helen nodded. "It's risky, but it might be our best chance. I'll need to gather the other Queens, the Sages. We'll need all the power we can muster."

As they discussed the logistics of the plan, Leah felt the weight of the Librarian's deadline pressing down on her. The eye in her palm pulsed like a ticking clock.

"Helen," she said, cutting through the discussion.

"There's something else you should know." Leah took a deep breath. "When we were in the library, I... I had to make a deal. The Librarian wasn't too pleased the scroll was taken, so they almost took me."

Helen's expression sharpened. "What kind of deal?"

Leah swallowed hard. "I have three days to return the scroll to the Librarian. If I don't..."

Helen let out a slow breath, her eyes softening. "Oh, Leah." She exhaled. "What have you done?"

"What I had to," Leah said. "But it means we need this to work."

Helen was quiet for a long moment, her gaze distant. "Then we'd better get to work. I'll call an emergency meeting. Go gather everyone we can trust. We move on Legion as soon as possible."

As Helen stood to leave, Leah caught her arm. "Helen," she whispered. "If this doesn't work... if we can't get the scroll in time..."

For a moment, Leah saw a glimpse of the mentor she'd known before everything went to hell. "We'll get it back, Leah. But if things turn sideways," she placed a hand on Leah's shoulder, her grip firm. "I'll do everything in my power to rescue you from that place. I promise."

"Thank you, Queen Helen," Lean said, looking down at her feet.

CHAPTER 30

FORTUNE

A weathered multi-residential unit loomed ahead of Leah and her friends in the darkness. The building sat just inside the newly erected barbed wire fence that marked the boundary between the Mystic camp and Sekrè Fami proper. Rusted metal coils caught the dim streetlights, casting spiraled shadows across the brick facade.

It was a far cry from their canvas tent in the heart of the camp, and being this close to the town's edge made her skin prickle. She glanced back at Sarah and Isaac as they walked the narrow strip between the fence and the building, catching the same worry she felt coiling in her gut.

A stocky Bishop with a shaved head and long beard stood guard at the door, his white cloak pristine despite the chaos that had engulfed the camp. As they approached, his eyes flashed yellow with *Tiferet* as he scanned them.

"This way," he grunted, pushing open the heavy wooden door.

Leah stepped inside, and the musty scent of disuse hit her nostrils. The interior was sparse—a small living room connected to an even smaller kitchen, with two doors leading to what she assumed were bedrooms. The furniture was a far cry from the comfort of their tent, but at least it had solid walls.

"I'll get a guard to bring you some dinner," the Bishop said, his hand still on the doorknob. "I'll be standing guard outside if you need anything."

"Wait!" Leah called out, her thoughts collecting over everything that'd happened in the last few hours. "My Squares. Can we see the surviving Squares?"

His brow furrowed. "Most have been evacuated. The only ones left here are still recovering."

"That's fine." Leah walked toward the door. "I'll pay them a visit. I'm sure they—"

The Bishop's bulky frame blocked her path. "I'm afraid I can't let you. The Queens instructed us to keep you three here for your safety."

Leah's eyes narrowed. "Our safety?"

The Bishop looked at the ground as he cleared his throat. "Miss, I'm just following orders."

Suspicion gnawed at Leah's gut. She activated *Tiferet*, her vision sharpening as she scanned her surroundings. Multiple bodies glowed with inner light, hidden in the bushes and shadows around the entrance.

"I see Jan Xie wants to keep us locked away," she muttered through a clenched jaw.

"This is for your protection, miss," the Bishop insisted.

As he turned to leave, Leah reached out, grabbing his arm. "Wait! Could I at least get a list of the casualties and injured? I want to know if my Squares are okay."

The Bishop pulled his arm back slowly. "I'll see what I can do."

With that, he stepped outside and closed the door behind him. Leah heard the click of a lock engaging.

She stood there, frozen, her mind reeling. Had she really

caused all of this? If her Squares were dead, could she forgive herself?

A gentle hand on her shoulder pulled her from the spiral. "Come on," Sarah said. "We need to make a plan."

Sarah guided her to the small living room, where they all sank onto a worn couch. For a long moment, no one spoke.

Isaac moved to the kitchenette. The clink of glasses and running water broke the stillness. He returned with glasses of water, the cool liquid soothing Leah's throat.

As she set the glass on the rickety coffee table, her gaze fell on her palm. The black eye blinked open momentarily, darting left and right before closing again.

"So, we have three days?" Isaac asked, his voice gentle but probing.

Leah nodded. "I didn't have much of a choice. They were going to keep me there forever, but then Asmodeus helped."

"Forever?" Sarah asked. "Why? I thought that thing had rules?"

Isaac crossed his arms. "It has to do with your mom, right?"

"It does. Apparently, they believe in blood debt."

"At least Queen Helen is on the same page," Isaac said. "I just wish we didn't have to rush this."

"I know," Leah said. "But it was this or an eternity in the library."

"We just need to get Legion in time," Isaac said. "We've been in worse situations."

"Yeah," Sarah laughed. "If we weren't on the brink of some kind of catastrophe, then I don't know who we are."

Leah let out a laugh. "You're not wrong."

A sharp knock at the door made them all jump. Sarah started to rise, but Leah stood first.

"I'll get it."

She approached the door cautiously until she heard the lock on the other side click. When she opened it, she found the Bishop standing there, his arms laden with Styrofoam containers and plastic bags.

"Kitchens were closed, so I got you some Chinese instead. And some new uniforms," he said.

Leah took the bags and containers, and the smell of food made her stomach growl. "Did you find out anything about the injured Squares?"

The Bishop shook his head. "I'm sorry."

Frustration bubbled up in Leah's chest. "Did you at least try?"

The Bishop's lips tightened into a thin line. "Good night, Black Knight Ackerman." He closed the door, sliding the outside lock into place.

"Those bastards," she snarled as she stomped into the living room. "How hard can it be to check that? This has to be Jan Xie trying to get back at me for something she doesn't even understand."

Sarah's eyes flashed with a familiar fire. "So, then we sneak out. If you use *Thagirion,* they can't stop us."

"That won't work," Isaac countered, reaching for one of the cardboard takeout boxes. "We're surrounded by Mystics. They'll notice our essence disappearing as soon as we become invisible. Even if Leah goes alone, they'll see someone missing."

Sarah's eyes flashed yellow as she peered beyond the walls. "Fuckers," she muttered under her breath.

Leah placed the food on the coffee table and plopped on the couch, rubbing her temples. "I have to know if they made it. I should've just asked Helen about it during our meeting. She would have helped."

Asmodeus's voice whispered in the back of her mind,

uncharacteristically gentle. *What's done is done. We must pick our battles if we wish to see this through in time.*

She knew he was right. But it still clawed at her, knowing that others blamed her for the attack.

Isaac slid a takeout container toward her. "You should have some food, Leah. We need to eat and rest. There's nothing else we can do now."

Leah's stomach growled as she grabbed a box, opened it, and took in the smell of barbecue and garlic noodles. Her mouth watered, but she noticed the pale meat and paused.

"Everything alright?" Sarah asked, taking a forkful of orange chicken.

Leah closed the box. "It's pork."

"Oh, right!" Sarah said, handing over her box of orange chicken and grabbing Leah's. "Sorry, I wasn't thinking."

"Are you sure?" Leah asked.

"I'll eat anything," Sarah said before stuffing the pork into her mouth.

When they finished, the empty takeout containers lay scattered across the table. Isaac leaned back, rubbing his belly. "I feel like I haven't eaten in days."

"You haven't." Leah shrugged. "Technically."

"Now that we aren't hangry," Sarah said. "What do you think Queen Helen is going to do?"

Isaac thought momentarily, then said, "Gather an army of trusted Mystics and Sages."

"I wonder if she'll include Madeline and Nykima," Leah said.

Sarah shook her head. "Doubt it. We just got attacked. I don't see Helen trusting rootworkers at the moment."

Isaac reached for one of the fortune cookies, waving it in the air. "True, but if we can have one of those protective circles Nykima created around the perimeter of the area of the trap, then that will bring us extra protection. Plus, he won't be able to escape."

Leah grabbed her own cookie, turning it over as she spoke. "But if he gets someone, or something, in that circle, he'll just sacrifice them and make a portal out of there."

Sarah cracked open her fortune cookie and bit off half. She unfolded the small slip of paper inside, reading aloud between chews.

"An old lover will come back to you." She rolled her eyes and tossed the paper onto the table.

"Ha, well, that's oddly accurate," Isaac pointed out. "Yuki should be—"

Sarah's sharp glare cut him off mid-sentence. Her nostrils flared as she spoke, her voice tight.

"She isn't an old lover. It was just a fling. She made that clear."

"You know you can talk to us about it," Leah said softly.

"I'm fine," Sarah said. She nodded to Leah's unopened cookie. "What's yours say?"

Leah cracked open her cookie and unfolded the slip of paper inside. "True friends will always surround you."

Sarah snorted. "Why are these things always so corny?"

Isaac wrapped an arm around Sarah. "Aw, you don't think it's cute?" he squeezed her tighter.

"Let. Me. Go," Sarah grunted, pushing against his hug. "You sappy little shit."

They burst out laughing. Leah joined in, wrapping her arms around Sarah and squeezing until they were all in tears.

"Read yours, Isaac!" Sarah said, slipping out from between the two of them.

Isaac bit into his cookie with gusto, chewing quickly. He cleared his throat dramatically before reading.

"Live this day as if it were your last."

The laughter died abruptly, silence filling the air.

"Oh." Isaac's face paled, and he reached for another cookie. "I'll just have another one." He cracked it open, pulled out the paper, and read aloud, "Help! I'm being held prisoner in a fortune cookie factory."

Sarah laughed. "Good one. Guess if we get out of this, we can go find whoever wrote that next."

Leah joined in on the laughter, her worries fading away. If only for a minute.

CHAPTER 31
SATARIEL

Leah tossed and turned in the narrow bed, her mind racing. The scratchy blanket tangled around her legs as she shifted, trying to find a comfortable position. But comfort seemed impossible when her thoughts circled back to her Squares, their faces flashing behind her closed eyelids.

You need to rest, Asmodeus's voice murmured in her mind.

Leah sighed, opening her eyes to stare at the cracked ceiling. "I can't. Not when I don't know if they're okay."

She could feel Asmodeus's frustration mirroring her own. For a moment, silence stretched between them. Then, hesitantly, the demon spoke again.

There might be a way.

Leah sat up. "What do you mean?"

I've been thinking of the copy of you we made.

Leah nodded. "Think we should use it again?"

Better now than during battle, Asmodeus said.

Leah swung her legs over the side of the bed, her bare feet touching the cold floor. "Do you think they'd notice?"

If we were quick about it, they would still see the three essences here while one of you escaped with Thagirion.

Leah stood and paced the small room. "Should we tell someone? What if something goes wrong?"

If we tell anyone, they'll either forbid its use or require vigorous training before trusting us to use it right, Asmodeus said. *I'd rather you see the Squares now so I can get some sleep.*

Leah stopped pacing, her gaze falling on Sarah's sleeping form in the bed across from hers. Through the thin wall, she could hear Isaac's soft snoring from the adjacent room where he slept. She took a deep breath.

"Fine. Let's do it. What do I do? Do you remember?"

Close your eyes and focus on the feeling from the alley. Remember how it felt to split yourself.

Leah did as instructed. With her eyes closed, she imagined those strange flames, focusing on the green one. As she did, she felt Asmodeus reaching for it and heard a faint echo in the back of her head; *Satariel.*

At first, nothing happened. Then, a tingling sensation spread through her body. It started in her chest and radiated outward until her skin felt like it was buzzing with electricity.

That's it, Asmodeus encouraged. Now, imagine stepping backward without actually doing it.

Leah concentrated, imagining herself stepping out of her own body. For a moment, vertigo overwhelmed her. She swayed, gripping the edge of the bed to steady herself. When she opened her eyes, she gasped.

There, standing in front of her, was herself. Leah looked down at her hands, flexing her fingers. She felt solid, real, and yet...

"It worked," she breathed, seeing herself out of both versions.

Now, quickly, Asmodeus urged. *Use Thagirion before anyone senses us.*

Leah nodded, imagining one of her calling on the familiar chill of invisibility. As she faded from view, she imagined her other self crawling back into bed.

She could feel herself pulling the covers up and closing her eyes as she eased the window open.

Once outside, Leah moved swiftly through the darkened camp. The few guards she passed never noticed her, their gazes sliding past her invisible form. As she approached the makeshift hospital, a knot formed in her stomach. What would she find inside?

Two nurses emerged from the building, lighting cigarettes as they stepped into the cool night air. Leah slipped past them, catching snippets of their conversation.

"...never seen anything like it," the taller one said. "That powder, it's nasty stuff."

The other nurse nodded grimly. "And to teenagers that young? I don't know if they'll make it."

Leah's blood ran cold. She waited, watching the nurses put out their cigarettes and step inside. Leah followed behind, moving deeper into the makeshift hospital. They passed by single rooms outfitted for Knights, Bishops, and Rooks. Then, they reached a set of doors and traveled down to a basement level.

The sight that greeted her nearly brought her to her knees.

Rows upon rows of beds filled an underground parking lot. And near the doors, her Squares. Jenna, Callum, Zoe, Ricky, and Ashley lay still, their skin ashen and sweat-covered. IVs dripped steadily into their arms.

Leah moved between the beds in a daze, her hand pressing against the cold foreheads of her Squares. When she reached Jenna, something inside her shattered.

She sank to the floor, doing everything to keep hold of *Thagirion* as she held back sobs. "I'm sorry," she whispered. "I'm so sorry. This is all my fault."

If she hadn't provoked the 1891 faction. If she'd been here to protect them.

Leah. Asmodeus's voice cut through her spiraling thoughts. *You couldn't have known.*

She shook her head, unable to speak through the tightness in her throat.

Listen to me, he pressed. *You know they were looking for any excuse to attack. It would have been something else if it hadn't been the boxing match. You couldn't have predicted their actions.*

"But I should have been here," Leah choked out.

You heard the nurses. They used some kind of powder. You'd be lying in one of these beds, too, unable to help anyone. We needed that information from the Library. Without it, we have no hope of stopping Legion.

Leah knew he was right, but the logic did little to ease the ache in her chest. She looked up at Jenna's pale face.

"They don't deserve this," she whispered.

They don't, Asmodeus agreed. *But wallowing in guilt won't help them. You've seen what you needed to, and now we must focus on defeating Legion. That's how we win this.*

Leah nodded, wiping away the tears that had formed in her eyes. She stood, taking one last look at her Squares.

"I'll make this right," she promised. "Somehow."

As she returned to her room, Leah crept back inside and neared her bed. As she did, the clone dissipated, merging back into her. She lay down in a warm bed, staring at the ceiling.

You need to rest, Asmodeus said again.

Leah sighed. "I don't know if I can. Not after seeing them like that."

There was a moment of hesitation, then Asmodeus spoke. *I could ease the burden if you'd let me.*

Leah frowned. "What do you mean?"

I can carry some of your emotions, he explained. *Not all of it. That wouldn't be healthy. But enough to let you sleep.*

Leah considered the offer. Exhaustion tugged at her, and she knew she needed to be at her best for whatever came next.

"Okay," she whispered. "Do it."

She felt a gentle pressure in her mind like cool fingers soothing away the sharp edges of her pain. The guilt and fear didn't disappear entirely, but they receded enough that she could breathe easier.

As her eyes grew heavy and she drifted away, Leah murmured, "Thank you."

CHAPTER 32

FOOL'S MATE

"Leah, wake up! We've got to go."

Leah's heart raced as she sat up, Isaac's whispers cutting through her fog of sleep.

She blinked, disoriented, as the past night's events came rushing back. Memories of her sneaking out to see her Squares, the gut-wrenching sight of their pale, unconscious forms. Guilt clawed at her.

"What's happening?" she croaked, pushing herself onto her elbows. The sun wasn't even up yet, the sky outside a dull grey.

Isaac let out a yawn as he turned in the doorway. "Emergency meeting. Helen's orders."

Sarah sat on the edge of her bed, tightening the laces to her boots. "Come on, sleepyhead! Lucky Isaac got you up. I was going to do ice water next."

Leah swung her legs over the side of the bed and yawned. "Did they say what it's about?"

"Nope." Sarah tossed Leah her uniform as Isaac turned away and rested his back on the doorframe. "But all the Queens are involved."

Leah stood and changed, and Isaac turned back around to catch her gaze. "You okay?" he asked. "You look like you hardly slept."

The words tumbled out of Leah before she could stop them. "I snuck out last night."

Sarah narrowed her eyes. "How? We had guards on us all night."

"I know. Asmodeus and I were trying something new. Something that could trick the guards."

"Lucky they didn't catch you," Isaac said. "Or they'd put us all in cells."

"Well, they didn't," Leah said. "And I saw what happened to my Squares. They're... it's bad, guys. It's some kind of powder that's making them sick."

Isaac nodded. "All the better reason to get to this meeting. The sooner we deal with Legion, the sooner we can get out of this place."

A familiar Scottish brogue cut through the morning chill as they stepped outside. "There you are!"

Jaime McMillan's broad smile contrasted his disheveled appearance, his long hair wild and beard unkempt. He limped down the steps and swept Leah into an unexpected but welcome hug.

"Good to see you alive, lassie," he said warmly.

"Is that relief I hear?" Leah managed a small smile.

"Maybe." Jaime's smile faded, the light in his eyes dimming as his jaw set. "But we've got work to do. Come on, they're waiting."

They entered the Queen's command center, stepping into a packed living room filled with high-ranking Mystics. Leah spotted Marcus Chance, one of the senior Black Rooks, peering over a map laid out on a table. Beside him, Eli paced back and forth, her fingers drumming anxiously against his thigh. The tension in the room was thick enough to cut. In the center of it all stood Helen, Micah, and Jan Xie, engaged in hushed conversation.

Helen looked up as they entered, her blue eyes meeting Leah's. "Good, you're here. We can begin."

Micah cleared his throat, commanding attention. "You've all been selected for a mission of utmost importance. Once we go over the brief, we will dispatch it immediately. Do you understand?"

"Yes, my Queen," everyone said in unison.

The wall-mounted screens flickered to life, showing live-streamed faces Leah recognized—the Sages who had scattered across the globe since the HQ attack. Yuki's pink hair stood out, as did Zafirah's intense gaze.

Helen stepped forward. "We've received intelligence on Legion's whereabouts. More importantly, we believe we can lure him out and potentially end this war once and for all."

Murmurs swept through the room.

Micah frowned and cleared his throat again, his voice straining to remain calm. "And why did you wait until now to mention this?"

"We defeated the biggest threat at the time with an ancient ritual neither of us had evidence of," Helen said. "Let's not pretend the Board hasn't buried countless secrets in the name of victory. Or shall we discuss your own collection of forbidden texts?"

Micah's jaw worked silently for a moment before he gave a sharp nod. "Fine, go on."

Helen looked back out at the crowd. "The scroll is no longer accessible, but the echo of that ritual still lingers in the place where it was performed. I believe we can use that residual energy to our advantage."

As Helen moved to the map table, Leah noticed that her

usual fluid movements seemed stiff, her face drawn with hidden pain. The Queen steadied herself against the table's edge before continuing.

"Years ago, the excommunicated Mystic, Elizabeth Mizrahi, and I performed a ritual that turned the war against Asmodeus. However, in doing so, we've learned that it had inadvertently led to Legion's rise in power. There was a scroll that we used, but it vanished when the ritual was over."

Helen's hand pressed against her side as she spoke, her voice tightening. When she caught Leah's concerned stare, she gave an almost imperceptible shake of her head—not now.

"What happens to this power once it's extracted?" Anat's voice cut through the tension. "Could it escape again? Or make an even worse Legion?"

Helen's gaze shifted to Leah. "We have contingencies in place."

The room erupted in murmurs until Micah stepped forward. "We understand your concerns. This is why we've selected each of you carefully. And why we've made certain arrangements—including having Nick remain behind as provisional Queen should the worst occur."

Leah nodded, somewhat surprised they wouldn't take him with them to help them heal, but the Squares and others in the makeshift hospital needed all the help they could get.

Jan Xie stepped forward and pointed to a spot on the map. "The ritual was performed here, in an abandoned processing factory in Chicago."

Micah produced a small box and began withdrawing chess pieces. Jan Xie's voice grew precise and sharp as Micah placed them on the map.

"Our defense will consist of three layers," she

explained, arranging the pieces. "Outer perimeter to engage any hostile forces, middle ring to maintain protective barriers and an inner circle where the ritual will take place."

"The Sages have been called to join us," Micah added. "They'll start securing the location and beginning preparations. Each of you will receive your specific assignments once we arrive. The positioning of every Mystic has been carefully calculated for maximum effectiveness."

"I will coordinate our overall strategy from the command center," Micah continued. "Jan Xie will oversee our defensive forces. Helen," he glanced at her with barely concealed concern, "will focus solely on the ritual with the Sages' support."

"And what about Legion?" a voice called from the back. "How can we be sure he'll come?"

Helen straightened, eyeing Leah. "We have an asset we'll be calling on. When the time comes, he will be drawn to the ritual site. Then, when we initiate the ritual, he won't be able to resist."

Leah found her mind drifting as they discussed positions, her hand pulsing as she felt the librarian's eye move beneath her skin.

"Leah." Helen's voice snapped her back to attention. "You have a crucial role to play in this."

Leah straightened, forcing herself to focus. "What do you need me to do?"

Helen pointed to the center of the map. "Your blood connection to Elizabeth makes you suited to help activate the ritual's echo. You'll be stationed here protected by our most powerful Mystics."

"And what about us?" Sarah asked, looking at the map. "We're not letting Leah go in there alone."

"She won't be alone," Micah said. "But you and your

Black Bishop friend will be on the perimeter. Your skills are needed to maintain our defensive line."

"That's bullsh—" Sarah began, but Isaac cut her off with a glance.

"With all due respect," Isaac said, his voice carefully controlled, "wouldn't it be safer to have us near Leah? In case something goes wrong?"

Jan Xie' glared. "Are you questioning the strategic decisions of your Queens, Black Bishop?"

The tension in the room ratcheted up several notches. Leah could feel Sarah bristling beside her, ready to explode.

"No," Leah said quickly, placing a calming hand on Sarah's arm. "We understand. We work best as a team."

Helen nodded. "I know this is difficult. But we need every Mystic in their optimal position if we're to have any chance of success."

A heavy silence fell over the room. Leah could feel the weight of countless eyes upon her, waiting to see how she'd react. She took a deep breath.

"I'll do whatever it takes to end this," she said.

Micah nodded approvingly. "Good. Now, there's one more matter to discuss. The inclusion of rootworkers. We've lost a bit of support from the faction uprising, but we still have sympathizers willing to help."

The room erupted into a flurry of whispers and protests. Jan Xie's voice cut through the chaos like a whip.

"Silence!" she barked. "This isn't up for debate. Former Mystic Nykima will join us in establishing protective circles around the warehouse."

"You can't be serious," a grizzled Black Rook near the back growled. "After what they did to the Squares?"

Leah felt a surge of anger. "That was the 1891 faction! Nykima had nothing to do with that attack," she snapped. "She's saved more Mystic lives than I can count."

The Rook opened his mouth to argue, but Helen raised a hand, silencing him. "This is not up for debate. Nykima's skills are invaluable, and if that is all the rootworkers will give us, then we will take that advantage."

Tension filled the room, but no one dared voice further objections.

"We move out immediately," Micah announced. "Helicopters are waiting to transport us to the airport. From there, we fly to Chicago." His gaze swept the room, landing on each face in turn. "This is our chance to end Legion's reign of terror once and for all. Failure is not an option."

As the room began to clear, Jaime caught Leah's eye across the room, giving her a subtle nod. It wasn't much, but it let her know he'd be there if anything turned sideways.

Then she felt a hand on her shoulder. She turned to find Helen staring back at her.

"A word, Leah. In private."

Leah nodded, following Helen into a small study off the main room. As soon as the door closed behind them, Helen's composure cracked, just for a moment.

"I know I'm asking a lot of you," she said, her voice barely above a whisper. "If there were any other way…"

Leah swallowed hard. "I understand."

Helen nodded, and a slight but proud smile grew on her face. "Your mother would be proud of you."

The words hit Leah hard in the gut, stirring up a whirlwind of emotions she'd been trying to keep buried. Before she could respond, there was a sharp knock at the door.

"It's time," Jan Xie's voice called out.

Helen straightened, her mask of authority sliding back into place. "Remember," she said, her voice low. "No matter what happens, trust your instincts."

As they returned to the bustling living room, Leah spotted Sarah and Isaac. She gave them what she hoped was a reassuring nod, even if she didn't believe it herself.

"Let's go," Micah announced, his voice carrying over the din. "Operation Fool's Mate begins now."

CHAPTER 33

THE LAST WITCH

The roar of helicopter blades sliced through the air as Leah approached four choppers waiting for them. Her heart hammered against her ribs. This was it. They finally had something to get at Legion.

Sarah fell into step beside her. "You ready for this?" she asked, shouting above the helicopter's whir.

Leah managed a tight nod. "As ready as I'll ever be."

Isaac joined them on Leah's other side, remaining silent.

They reached the first helicopter, where Helen stood conferring with a Black and White Knights cluster. The Queen's pale hair whipped around her face as she gave them instructions. When she caught sight of Leah, she broke away from the group.

"The Sages are already en route," Helen called over the noise. "We'll coordinate our arrival in stages to avoid drawing attention." She gestured to the helicopter. "You three are with me. We need to make contact with our asset before we arrive."

Leah nodded, pushing down the knot growing in her chest. "Understood."

They boarded the helicopter, finding Nykima already strapped in and her wheelchair secured nearby. Jaime McMillan climbed in after them, followed by Helen, who moved with careful, measured steps.

As the rotors spun to life, Leah caught a glimpse of Madeline approaching the helicopter and stopping in front of Helen. Her eyes gleamed an unnatural yellow as she mouthed something to the Queen.

Helen's face tightened with pain—whether from Madeline's words or her condition, Leah couldn't tell. Before she could process it, they were airborne, the ground falling away beneath them.

Helen's voice crackled through the headset. "Leah, I need you to contact Cora now. We can't afford any surprises. And we need her to work with us to get Legion to the factory. Alone if possible."

Leah nodded and took a deep breath, closing her eyes. She focused on the memory of Cora's office and the High Priestess's penetrating gaze. The helicopter's vibrations faded away, replaced by a sensation of falling through space.

She found herself seated across from Cora when she opened her eyes. The office looked the same as always, but there was a heaviness in the air.

"Welcome back," Cora said, her voice warm despite the weariness etched into her features.

"Cora," Leah breathed. "I... we're going to an old processing factory in Chicago. Helen wanted me to coordinate the timing."

Cora nodded. "What do you need?"

Leah relayed the plan, explaining the blood ritual Helen and her mother had performed years ago. As she spoke, she noticed a flicker of something in Cora's eyes. Recognition? Resignation?

"I see," Cora said when Leah finished. "I might be able to control him. But if I bring him to you, you're certain this will work?"

Leah hesitated. "It's our best shot. But that still leaves you. Once we defeat Legion, how will you escape?"

The High Priestess's expression softened, a sad smile playing at her lips. "Oh, I won't be."

"What?" Leah's voice cracked. "What do you mean? We can—there has to be a way."

Cora held up a hand, silencing Leah. "This place inside Legion is a void. The essence of my lost Immortal Witches has kept me safe, but to get Legion to you, I'll need to leave here. When I get a hold of him, you all won't have long. And once you take the core, this place will collapse along with everything else here."

"But—"

"But nothing. The collapse will be quick and painless."

Leah shook her head. "I don't understand. What about Frank? What about re-building the Immortal Witches?"

Cora smiled. "I've lived for thousands of years. The witches will rise again. They always do. But I cannot be their leader. I failed them. I ignored your and Queen Helen's warning."

"No," Leah whispered, tears stinging her eyes. "There has to be another way."

"If you are ever in doubt, find Frank. He's bound to stumble his way into making a new coven soon enough."

"I can't let you die." Leah's voice rose with anger and grief warring within her. "Haven't we lost enough? You have so much you could teach. We can't lose you."

Cora reached across the desk, taking Leah's hands in her own. "This is my choice. My penance."

Leah's shoulders slumped. "I don't know if I'm strong enough for this."

"You are," Cora said firmly. "You're stronger than you know. And you carry the strength of generations within you."

Leah frowned. "What do you mean?"

Cora's eyes looked distant as if peering into the past. "Did you know that I knew Judas Maccabeus?"

Leah blinked. "The... the leader of the Maccabees? From Hanukkah?"

Cora nodded, a fond smile playing on her lips. "He was a remarkable man. Stubborn as a mule, mind you, but with a spirit that could move mountains."

Leah wiped a tear and leaned forward. "You really knew him?"

"Oh yes," Cora chuckled. "We fought side by side against the Seleucid Empire. I saw firsthand the strength of the Jewish people, their refusal to bow to tyranny or abandon their faith."

"But what does that have to do with me?"

Cora eyed Leah. "Everything. That same blood, that same indomitable spirit, flows through your veins. When you face Legion, remember the Maccabees. Remember how they stood against an empire that sought to crush them, armed with nothing but faith and the courage of their convictions."

Leah swallowed hard. "I never thought about it like that."

"You should. Your ancestors fought battles that seemed impossible, Leah. They resisted assimilation and preserved their culture and beliefs against overwhelming odds. That strength is your birthright."

Tears welled in Leah's eyes again. "Thank you for that," she whispered.

Cora smiled. "Well, I've had a few thousand years to pick up some wisdom. Might as well share it while I can."

Leah and Cora laughed together momentarily. Then, a heavy silence settled over the office.

"It's time, isn't it?" Leah asked.

Cora nodded, rising from her chair. She circled the desk, pulling Leah into a tight embrace. "Remember what I've told you: when things seem dark, when you feel like you can't go on, look to your ancestors. Draw strength from their struggles, their triumphs. You are part of a legacy that stretches back thousands of years. Never forget that."

Leah clung to her. "I won't. I promise."

Cora pulled back, cupping Leah's face in her hands. "Now go. Face Legion with the courage of the Maccabees, with the strength of generations behind you."

As the office faded, Leah saw something in the windows behind Cora. A writhing darkness that seemed to watch with hungry eyes. But before she could focus on it, reality bled back in at the edges.

She blinked, finding herself back in the helicopter. Tears dampened her cheeks.

"You okay?" Sarah asked.

"Yeah," Leah said. "Yeah, I'm okay."

Helen turned back to look at her. "Did you get to her?"

Leah nodded. "Cora's ready. Once she brings him to us, we'll finally end this."

CHAPTER 34

PREPARATIONS

Leah gripped the private jet's armrest as they landed a second time. This flight wasn't as choppy as the helicopter they took to the small airport that housed the Queen's private jets, but the landing was definitely not smooth.

Sarah stirred beside her, letting out a loud yawn.

"Rise and shine, sleeping beauty," Leah murmured, nudging her friend.

Sarah groaned and wiped her face. "Are we there already?"

Isaac's voice drifted from across the aisle as he swiped a tablet. "Yep, pulling into the private hangers now."

Through the window, Leah spotted several other private jets parked, no doubt the Sages.

As they climbed off the plane, Leah's gaze swept over the stern-faced individuals in dark suits waiting on the tarmac. They were all Helen's bonded Knights and Bishops, waiting for them to arrive.

Micah strode forward, his voice carrying across the tarmac. "The Sages have secured the location. We move in convoy formation. Helen, you'll ride with me. The rest of you, to your assigned vehicles."

Leah fell into step beside Sarah and Isaac as they were ushered towards a line of sleek black SUVs.

As they climbed into one of the vehicles, Leah caught Helen's eye. The Queen leaned heavily on Micah's arm. Something flickered across her expression. Nostalgia? Regret? Leah couldn't place it, but the Queen disappeared into the car, and Leah got into hers.

The drive through Chicago's bustling streets felt surreal. She'd been a different person the last time she was here. Someone else entirely. As they passed the Chicago University campus, she recalled how often she and her dad talked about her possibly going there one day.

"Look at them." Sarah watched a group of students crossing the street in front of them. "Just normal kids. No demons, no world-ending threats. Finals and frat parties."

Isaac leaned forward, his eyes fixed on another group of laughing students crossing the street. "I wonder what their biggest worry is right now. A tough professor? Relationship drama?"

Leah's throat tightened. "Definitely not whether they'll live to see tomorrow."

Silence fell over them, and Leah's mind drifted, imagining a world where their biggest concerns was holding Sarah back from shouting about unfair grading curves or pulling Isaac out of the library to go to a party.

"When this is all over, and Legion is gone," Sarah said suddenly, breaking the silence, "we should come back here and crash a party. Pretend to be normal."

Isaac laughed. "And how do you think we'll be able to do that? Unless they have a demon or something nearby, we'll never get to—"

"Then we steal a helicopter." Sarah grinned. "I don't

know. Please don't ruin my dreams. What about you, Leah? Are you in?"

Leah smiled. "You know what? Why not? But I'm not getting into a helicopter with you at the controls."

"Me too," Isaac said. "Once we kick Legion's ass, we party like... well, like normal people."

They laughed, the sound a bit forced but genuine, nonetheless. For a moment, Leah could almost believe in that future. In this world, they could finally celebrate instead of mourning all the loss.

The SUV turned off the main road and wound through an industrial area. Abandoned warehouses and crumbling factories loomed on either side.

"We're getting close," the driver announced.

Leah's heart rate picked up as she caught sight of their destination. The old, abandoned silos rose against the skyline, a collection of massive concrete towers standing sentinel over the surrounding wasteland. Graffiti covered the lower levels in bright colors layered over each other.

Something tickled at the back of Leah's mind. A sensation that prickled at the nape of her neck.

You're sensing it too, Asmodeus's voice rumbled in her head. *There's an energy here. Old. Powerful.*

As they drew closer, Leah noted Black Knights patrolling the perimeter, keeping the area secure.

The SUV stopped, and Leah took a deep breath, steeling herself for what would come. As they climbed out, she looked up at the silos, which stretched high into the sky.

Good vantage points, Asmodeus observed. *But something still feels off. Be wary.*

"I know," Leah whispered.

The sage of *Netzach*, Desmond Hawthorne, approached their group, his expression grave. His gaze settled on Sarah and Isaac. "You two, we need you with Nykima. She's setting up our defensive rings and specifically requested your assistance."

"What?" Sarah's head snapped toward Leah. "But we should—"

"Every position has been carefully chosen," Desmond cut in, his tone brooking no argument. "This isn't random. Your skills are crucial to maintaining the barriers that will keep Legion's forces at bay."

Leah's throat tightened, but she forced a smile. "Go. I'll be fine."

"Join them for now," Desmond said to Leah. "We'll call you in when we need you,"

They made their way over, careful not to disturb the intricate patterns Nykima was already laying down. The former Knight looked up as they approached, her face etched with concentration.

"We're doing two rings," she said. "One close to the building, another about forty feet out. I need you three to help me complete them."

Nykima handed them small bags that smelled awful.

"What's in it?" Isaac asked.

"Iron, salt, dried manure, and some other ingredients." Nykima grinned as Sarah held out her bag. "Once activated, it should slow down any demons Legion brings with him without him noticing."

"But it won't stop Legion? How?" Sarah asked, following behind Nykima and carefully pouring a line of the silvery powder.

"That's what we hope. The second ring is a different mix that should keep him in. So, he'll be trapped without his army."

As they neared completion of the outer ring, Nykima looked at Sarah and Isaac. "Listen, I'm trusting you two to keep me safe during all this. If I go down, these barriers fall. Understand?"

Isaac nodded. "We won't let you down."

Jaime's voice called out behind them. "Leah! Time to go, lass. Helen needs you for the preparations. Sarah, you, too."

The moment Leah had been dreading had arrived. She turned to her friends. "Good luck."

Sarah was the first to move, enveloping Leah in a fierce hug. "We're gonna kick his ass."

Isaac joined the embrace, his lanky arms encircling them both. "We've got your back."

As they pulled apart, Leah caught Nykima's eye. The former Knight gave her a slight nod. "For Eric," Nykima said softly.

Leah winced, a flood of emotion threatening to surface at the mention of her uncle. "For Eric," she agreed. "For all of them."

With one last look at Sarah and Isaac, Leah turned and walked towards Jaime, standing tall.

CHAPTER 35

THE BLOOD RITUAL

The abandoned silos loomed ahead like some hulking beast, its corroded walls catching the dim light as Leah approached with Jaime.

Leah's chest tightened as she glanced back, catching a glimpse of her friends helping Nykima complete the outer ring. Part of her ached to be with them, but she knew they each had their role to play.

"Ready, lass?" Jaime asked, his Scottish brogue gentle as he shifted his weight off his bad leg.

Leah stood tall. "Legion's killed too many people we care about. He's not taking anyone else without a fight."

"Good. Here we are." Jaime limped to a stop before the silo's rusted doors.

The words Leah wanted to say to her friends lodged in her chest, but there was no time for second thoughts now. She had to trust they would do their part while she did hers.

The warehouse doors groaned open, releasing a wave of warm air tinged with a strange feeling that put Leah's teeth on edge. Inside, dozens of Mystics moved through the cavernous space, drawing symbols on weapons that glowed with dull energy.

Through the crowd of white and black cloaks, a flash of vivid pink caught Leah's attention. Yuki wove between the busy Mystics, her usual bouncing stride subdued. Dark circles shadowed her eyes, and her signature pink hair had grown out, revealing dark roots.

"There you are," Yuki said, her voice tight as she approached. "Helen's looking for you."

Leah frowned at the sage's drawn expression. "Everything okay?"

Yuki glanced around the bustling space, then leaned in close. "It's a mess. Desmond wants half the Sages stationed outside. Says we need a strong perimeter defense, but..." She trailed off, biting her lip.

"But what?" Leah pressed.

"It feels wrong," Yuki admitted. "We should all be in here, combined strength and all that. I don't like how spread out we are."

She has a point, Asmodeus's voice rumbled in Leah's mind. *This positioning leaves us vulnerable.*

Before Leah could respond, Helen's voice rang out across the warehouse. "Leah! Over here."

Near the middle of the space, Helen stood with Eli and Zafirah, standing around strange markings on the floor that seemed untouched by the graffiti that marked everywhere else. Helen's usual commanding presence seemed diminished as she clutched her side, her face pale beneath her composure.

Leah squeezed Yuki's arm. "We'll talk more later, okay?"

Making her way through the crowd, Leah felt the air grow heavier with each step toward the ritual site. The hair on the back of her neck stood up as she recognized some of the same markings from the library's scroll. Their shapes seemed to writhe at the edge of her vision.

"Good," Helen said, her voice strained as Leah approached. "We need to go over the ritual."

Helen gestured to the center of the pattern, where an oval shape contained a distinct handprint and markings Leah knew translated to "Ethereal." The symbols pulsed with a dull red light, making the air feel charged and electric.

"This is where you'll stand." Helen handed Leah a small knife. "When the time comes, you'll need to add your blood here."

"And that will activate the ritual?" Leah asked, studying the complex design as it seemed to dance beneath her feet.

Helen nodded. "Elizabeth was the one who performed this part, so your blood connection to her should resonate with the latent energy. That should create a beacon for Legion's ethereal side to notice."

Leah's stomach churned. "And then what? How are we going to pull it out of him?"

"Well," Eli interjected, his monotone voice at odds with how Leah felt. "The ritual creates a sort of tether. But extracting the core will take immense power and precision."

"Which is where we come in," Zafirah added. Even from several feet away, heat waves rolled off her skin, making the air shimmer.

Leah looked between them, noting the tension in their postures. "What if it's not enough?" she asked, Asmodeus's concerns bubbling to the surface alongside hers. "What's our backup plan?"

Helen's eyes narrowed slightly. "We have contingencies in place. If the ritual fails, we move to direct confrontation. Every Mystic here is prepared to give their all."

"And if that's not enough?" Leah pressed.

"Then we have a final option," Helen said. "A last resort that only Micah can initiate. But let's pray it doesn't come to that."

Leah clenched her jaw, but before she could push further, a sudden, searing pain lanced through her head. She gasped, stumbling backward as the warehouse around her blurred.

A familiar voice echoed in her mind. *Leah!* Cora shouted. *I've got him! He's coming. I'm bringing him to you, but I can't hold him for long.*

The pain receded as quickly as it had come. Leah blinked, surrounded by concerned faces, the ritual marks pulsing more intensely at her feet.

"What happened?" Eli demanded. "What did you see?"

Leah swallowed hard, her mouth dry. "It's Cora. She says Legion is coming. Now."

Helen straightened, her voice ringing out with renewed authority despite her obvious pain. "Everyone to your positions! This is not a drill. I repeat, to your positions! Legion is coming!"

CHAINS

Leah crouched in the shadows of the warehouse, her heart thundering against her ribs as she counted the seconds until Legion's arrival. Around her, dozens of hidden Mystics held their breath, waiting to spring their trap. The last vestiges of light filtered through grimy skylights above, casting long shadows across the ritual circle at the center of the cavernous space. Ancient symbols marked into the concrete floor, writing and shifting in the dim light, as if waiting for Leah's blood to awaken them.

She felt Asmodeus's presence stirring within her, an unease that mirrored her own.

Are you ready for this?

Leah swallowed hard, her fingers unconsciously tracing the outline of the Librarian's eye embedded in her palm. "As ready as I'll ever be," she murmured back.

Helen's voice carried in a whisper through the darkness. "Remember, we have one chance. Once Cora guides him in here, we must act as one to hold him."

The warehouse doors groaned open, and a figure stumbled inside. Leah's breath caught as she recognized Legion's form, still wearing Reginald Platt's face, but his eyes blazed an unnatural purple. His movements were jerky and unnatural, like a marionette fighting its strings.

"Ethereal... demon... human..." Legion's voice shifted between tones, sometimes deep and guttural, other times almost feminine, like Cora speaking through him. "Need to bind everything back. Yes, yes, this will work."

Leah's muscles tensed as Legion lurched closer to the ritual circle. She locked eyes with Helen across the room, waiting for the signal. The Queen gave an almost imperceptible nod when Legion stepped deep enough inside.

"Now!" Helen's voice rang out.

Leah activated *Thagirion*, the familiar chill of invisibility washing over her as she darted toward the ritual circle. Around her, the hidden Mystics emerged in perfect coordination. Jaime's voice boomed out, leading the first wave of *Hod*.

"What is this?" Legion snarled, his movements slowing as the power took hold. "You dare to—"

His words cut off as more Mystics joined the effort, layers of *Hod* pressing down on him from all directions. Knights and Bishops moved in practiced formation, each adding strength to hold him in place.

Leah pulled the knife Helen gate her as she reached the ritual circle. The symbols pulsed faintly, recognizing Elizabeth's blood in her veins.

"Quickly, Leah!" Helen's voice strained with effort. "We can't hold him for long!"

Leah gritted her teeth and dragged the blade across her forearm. Blood welled up, bright red against her skin. She held her arm over the intricate markings, watching droplets fall onto the symbols. The moment her blood touched the ground, the entire circle blazed to life with deep crimson light, pulsing in time with her racing heart.

"It's working!" Jaime called out.

Legion's violet eyes flickered between purple and dark as Cora's control wavered. He strained against *Hod*, letting out a sonorous bellow that shook the dust from the rafters. Black chains erupted from his body, writhing and snapping like serpents.

"Hold him!" Jaime roared. "Don't let those chains touch you!"

Leah pressed her bleeding palm to the center of the circle, feeling her energy flow into the ritual. The symbols blazed brighter, and suddenly, red chains of pure energy burst forth from the ground. They lashed out with deadly precision, piercing Legion's chest and wrapping around something bright within him. The ethereal core.

Legion's shriek was a symphony of voices, human and demon and something else entirely. "No! You can't have it!"

The air crackled with power as Legion's black chains wrapped around the red ones, trying to hold the core in place. But the ritual's chains held true, slowly pulling the glowing sphere from his chest.

"Almost there," Helen called out, triumph creeping into her voice. "Just a little more!"

A deafening crash shattered the moment. Shards of glass rained down as two figures plummeted through the skylight. Leah's eyes widened in shock as she recognized Sandeep and Nona, the missing Sages.

Time seemed to slow to a crawl. Leah watched, helpless, as Nona's eyes blazed with an unnatural light, seeing through her *Thagirion* shield. The Sage's gaze locked onto her.

"No!" Leah gasped, realizing what was happening was too late.

Nona's arm shot out, a blade of pure force hurtling toward Leah with deadly precision. Leah tried to dodge, but her reactions were sluggish from blood loss and shock. She could only watch as the *Malchut* blade came flying toward her.

CHAPTER 37

DARK SAGES

Leah's world exploded in a blur of motion and searing pain as Helen appeared beside her, clamping onto her arm. The silo's interior vanished in a dizzying rush, that familiar sensation of being squeezed through a tight tunnel. They materialized atop one of the massive grain hoppers near the silo's peak, giving Leah a perfect view of the chaos below.

"Stay still," Helen commanded, her voice strained as she pressed her palm to Leah's bleeding shoulder. Warmth flowed from the Queen's touch, knitting flesh and easing the agony of Nona's attack. Through the maze of industrial machinery and catwalks, Leah could see the Mystics maintaining their positions outside, the fire illuminating the mass of demons slowed by Nykima's circles.

Blood trickled from Helen's nose.

"You're hurt," Leah said.

"It's nothing,'" Helen said, wiping her nose, her face ashen. "We need to get back down there. The ritual—"

A deafening crack split the air. The glowing red chains of the ritual disintegrated like mist, leaving only scorched concrete and fractured symbols. Below, Legion's laughter echoed off the curved walls as the exposed core glowed brightly from his chest.

"No time," Helen gasped. "Plan B. Ready?"

Leah nodded, and they leaped from the hopper, Helen's teleportation bringing them to the heart of the chaos. The silo's interior had become a war zone. Mystics and corrupted Sages clashed between old machinery, powers flaring in the dusty air. Through a crumbling wall, Leah glimpsed more Knights rushing to reinforce their position, their cloaks billowing as they fought through waves of Legion's demons.

Sandeep's *Hod* hold had frozen a group of Knights against a rusted grain chute. Leah didn't hesitate. She channeled *Malchut*, the force push catching the corrupted Sage off guard. He flew backward, crashing into the wall as the freed Knights rejoined the battle.

The ritual circle, Asmodeus urged.

Leah sprinted to where the ritual had been, her heart sinking at the destruction. Nothing remained of the intricate symbols except scorched concrete and spiderweb cracks.

You know what this means, Asmodeus growled.

"Yeah." Leah's fists clenched as she turned to face Legion, eyeing the still-exposed core. "We fight."

The monster before her barely resembled Reginald Platt now. Black chains writhed from his expanding form, smashing through support beams and wrapping around the silo's curved walls. The ethereal core pulsed within his grotesquely distorted chest.

Leah drew on multiple wells simultaneously, *Malchut* crackling around her fists as she launched forward. *Gevurah* flames erupted from her palms as she landed the first strikes. A massive chain whipped toward her head, but Asmodeus took control, using *Nehemoth* to pull them aside mid-air. The chain scraped past, taking chunks of concrete from the wall behind them.

Through another breach in the silo wall, Leah caught glimpses of the larger battle—fires consuming nearby structures, Mystics locked in desperate combat, Nykima's protective circles barely holding as more demons slipped through.

Leah pressed her attack, combining *Malchut*-enhanced strikes with bursts of flame. Legion roared, more in anger than pain, as portions of his corrupted flesh burned away.

"Insolent child!"

Chains erupted from every part of him now. Leah called on *Netzach*, feeling strikes bounce off her invulnerable form as she dove and rolled. She came up in a crouch, panting, as Legion's form began to shift and grow.

"Your precious tree will be mine!" His voice boomed in a cacophony of tones that set her teeth on edge. "Once I've devoured every last one of you, pathetic creatures."

The core pulsed brighter, and Leah felt a sickening lurch in her stomach. He was regaining control, drawing the power deeper into himself. Sinew started to stretch and wrap around the core, closing it off.

No! Asmodeus snarled. *We can't let him—*

Leah launched another set of attacks, joining mystics as they threw *Malchut* slices at him, tearing into his chest.

"Enough!" Legion's roar shook the entire structure. A wave of telekinetic force exploded outward, hurling Leah and the other Mystics back. She slammed into a support beam, stars exploding behind her eyes as Legion's massive form spun.

Chains whirled like the blades of some nightmarish helicopter, tearing through everything in their path. The silo's walls shattered, raining debris as support beams groaned and snapped.

The being before her now towered fifteen feet high, its body a writhing mass of chains, eyes, and pulsing darkness. Six wings unfurled from its back as the ethereal core blazed at its center like a captured star.

"Behold," Legion's voice boomed, "the true face of your destroyer!"

A tendril lashed out, morphing into a wickedly sharp claw.

Leah's tired muscles screamed as she launched forward, calling on her remaining power. If she could just reach the core—

Pain exploded in her side as Nona appeared through the chaos, her *Malchut* blade slicing through the air. Leah tumbled to the ground, gasping as she clutched her bleeding side as Legion loomed over her.

"It's time," Legion growled, "for you to finally die."

A chain wrapped around Leah's ankle, dragging her closer. She looked up into Legion's grotesque face, saw the claw descending toward her chest, and knew with sickening certainty that she'd failed.

I'm sorry, she thought, closing her eyes as the claw plunged downward.

CHAPTER 38

DEATH

Searing pain exploded in Leah's mind as Legion's massive claw tore through her chest. Blood filled her mouth and her vision swam as she crumpled to the ground. Through the haze of agony, she caught glimpses of the battle raging around her—Zafirah's flames illuminating the warehouse in bursts of orange light, Desmond racing toward Legion as chains bounced off him, Yuki's crackling energy blasts peppering the monster's grotesque body.

"Leah!" Yuki's panicked voice cut through the chaos. "Hold on!"

Legion pulled back, the Sages tearing into him too much to keep his focus on her.

Leah tried to respond but only managed a wet cough that splattered more blood across the concrete. Her fingers scrabbled weakly at the gaping wound in her chest, feeling warm liquid pulsing between them with each labored heartbeat.

This is it, she thought dimly. *After everything, this is how it ends.*

Don't you dare give up, Asmodeus growled in her mind. *We're not dying here.*

A familiar figure appeared in Leah's blurring vision. Eli stood above her, his usually impassive face etched with concern as he knelt beside her.

"Stay with me," he muttered, his hands pressing on her and sending warmth into her.

Chesed filled her, knitting flesh and bone back together. Leah gritted her teeth against a fresh wave of pain. She focused on Eli's face, using it as an anchor to cling to consciousness.

She saw movement behind him. Sandeep. He stood there, smiling.

"Behind you," she tried to warn, but the words came out as little more than a gurgle.

Eli's body went rigid. His healing abruptly cut off as *Hod* took hold. Sandeep stepped forward, grinning as he stood behind Eli.

"I've been waiting for this moment," the corrupted Sage said. "The great Eli Abrams forgetting to watch his own back."

Eli strained against the invisible bonds holding him in place, his lips turning blue, but Sandeep's *Hod* was too strong. "Why?" Eli managed. "We trusted you."

Sandeep's smile widened. "Because sometimes, old foundations must fall to create a better world. Legion will remake everything and purge the corruption."

"You're insane," Leah croaked, struggling to push herself up despite the agony lancing through her chest.

Sandeep's gaze shifted to her. "And you, Leah Ackerman. The so-called hero. I've been curious to see what makes you so special." His hands came together, fingers forming the distinct shape used to channel *Malchut*. "Let's find out, shall we?"

Time seemed to slow as Leah watched the first *Malchut* bullet form between Sandeep's palms. She tried to move, to do anything, but her body refused to cooperate. All she could do was watch in helpless horror as Sandeep fired.

Eli let out a roar, pushing through Sandeep's *Hod* at the last minute, creating a barrier between him and Leah. The bullet tore through Eli's back, emerging in a spray of blood from his chest. Eli's eyes went wide with shock and pain, a choked gasp escaping his lips. But Sandeep wasn't finished. A second bullet followed, then a third, each impact jerking Eli's body like a macabre puppet.

"No!" Leah screamed, the sound tearing at her raw throat. She reached for her powers, desperate to stop this, but found only emptiness. She was too weak, too drained from her injuries.

The fourth bullet went wide, striking Leah's leg. Fresh agony exploded through her, momentarily whiting out her vision. When it cleared, she found Eli's glassy eyes fixed on her face. Blood trickled from the corner of his mouth as he struggled to speak.

"I'm... sorry," he wheezed. "I should have..."

"No," Leah sobbed, reaching for him despite the pain. "Please, hold on. We'll fix this. We'll—"

But Eli's eyes were already growing distant, the light fading from them with each ragged breath. Sandeep stood over them both, his expression one of clinical detachment as he watched Eli's life slip away.

"Fascinating," he mused. "Even now, he tries to protect you. What loyalty you inspire."

Rage, unlike anything Leah had ever felt before, surged through her, temporarily drowning out the pain of her injuries. She glared up at Sandeep, wishing she had the strength to tear him apart with her bare hands. She strained to push herself up, but Sandeep simply wagged his finger, and she was frozen in place.

"I'll kill you," she snarled. "I swear, I'll make you pay for this."

Sandeep raised an eyebrow. "Bold words from someone bleeding out on the floor. But I'm afraid your story ends here. Take comfort in knowing your death will serve a greater purpose."

As Sandeep raised his hands to deliver the final blow, Leah felt Asmodeus stir deep within her.

With nothing left to lose, Leah surrendered herself to his power. Green flames erupted around her body, searing away the pain and filling her with impossible strength. She felt herself splitting, one version remaining on the ground while another materialized behind Sandeep.

The corrupted Sage's eyes widened in shock as he spun to face this new threat. "How—?"

Leah didn't give him a chance to finish. She reached deep within herself, tapping into a well of power she'd never accessed before. *Samael* answered her call, flooding her with dark energy that made her previous uses of the Tree of Death seem like child's play.

She lunged forward, her hand closing around Sandeep's throat. The moment they connected, she felt his life force flowing into her. His skin grew pale and withered as Leah's wounds closed, the shattered bones and torn flesh knitting back together.

"What... how?" Sandeep gasped, clawing weakly at her grip.

Leah's eyes blazed, a hunger inside growing, needing to devour this man entirely. "You get exactly what you deserve," she growled, her voice distorted and inhuman.

She poured more of *Samael*'s power into the connection, draining Sandeep's essence faster and faster. His struggles grew feeble, his eyes sunken, and his skin stretched tight across his bones. Leah knew she should stop, that this level of power was dangerous, but neither she nor Asmodeus wanted to.

Only when Sandeep's body had shriveled to a desiccated husk did Leah finally release him. He crumpled to the ground, nothing more than a withered corpse. Leah stood over him, chest heaving as the green flames and dark energy receded.

Reality crashed back in as the two versions of herself merged once more. The sounds of battle filled her ears. Legion roared before her, fending off fire as people screamed around him. But all Leah could focus on was Eli's broken body.

She stumbled to his side, gathering his head into her arms. "No, no, no," she muttered, her hands glowing as she tried to channel *Chesed*. "Come on, Eli. Don't do this. Don't leave us."

But it was too late. Eli stared up at her, his eyes glassy and lifeless. As Leah cradled him, she noticed something that made her heart clench—a small, genuine smile on Eli's face.

"I'm sorry," she whispered, tears streaming down her face. "I'm so sorry I couldn't save you."

CHAPTER 39

BINAH

Eli's lifeless form looked up at her as Leah knelt motionless. The chaos of battle raged around her, but it all felt like it was somewhere else. She was hollow. Another life gone in front of her.

"Leah!" Jaime's voice cut through the fog. "We need you! Now!"

She turned, her movements mechanical, to see the Rook fending off a possessed Black Knight. The barriers must have fallen. The Knight grinned at her, his movements jerky and uncoordinated as he launched himself at Jaime.

Without conscious thought, Leah felt the familiar surge of green flames engulfing her body. A copy of Leah materialized beside the possessed Knight, green flames dancing across her skin. The clone moved with lightning speed, a *Malchut* blade forming in her hand as she struck. The Knight crumpled to the ground.

"Bloody hell," Jaime breathed, his eyes wide. "How did you—"

"*Satariel,*" Leah and her clone said in unison, their voices overlapping in an unsettling echo. "This well... it's something else."

As quickly as it had appeared, the clone dissipated into wisps of green flame. Leah stumbled, a wave of dizziness washing over her as she reintegrated.

Across the warehouse, Jan Xie's voice rang out in a furious battle cry. Leah spun to see the Black Queen locked in combat with Nona, blue flames erupting from her hands. The corrupted Sage dodged and weaved, but Jan Xie pressed her advantage relentlessly.

"You were supposed to protect us!" Jan Xie snarled, her attacks growing more ferocious.

Nona laughed, the sound harsh and distorted. "We serve a higher purpose now. Legion will—"

Her words cut off in a choked gasp as Jan Xie's flames finally found their mark. The blue fire engulfed Nona, searing through her *Netzach* defenses. Leah watched in horrified fascination as the Sage's skin blackened and cracked, her screams fading to whimpers before she collapsed into a charred husk.

A deafening roar shook the warehouse. Legion's strange form writhed, twisting and expanding. Chains tore from his flesh and slashed about in the open air. His torso split open, revealing row upon row of razor-sharp teeth.

"I will devour you all!" Legion's voice boomed, a cacophony of tones that set Leah's teeth on edge.

As the massive maw opened wide, preparing to unleash devastation, a blur of motion caught Leah's attention. Micah propelled himself forward.

"Now, Helen!" the White Queen shouted.

Helen's voice rang out, clear and commanding. "Everyone, brace yourselves!"

Micah's hand shot out, fingertips barely grazing Legion's grotesque snout. In that instant, everything froze. Legion's massive form hung suspended in mid-transformation, teeth half-formed, and chains arrested mid-lash. Micah was equally motionless, caught channeling a power Leah hadn't seen in action.

The air around them shimmered as *Binah,* the well of time, took hold. Leah watched in awe and horror as Micah's appearance changed. His salt-and-pepper hair turned stark white, then thinned. Deep lines etched themselves across his face, his skin taking on a papery quality.

"By the Tree," Jaime whispered. "He's sacrificing years of his life for this."

Leah's heart clenched at the sight. Unlike *Hod,* which couldn't hold Legion for long, Micah was giving up time to hold him. She knew they couldn't waste this opportunity. She sprinted towards Legion's frozen form, calling on every ounce of power she could muster.

"Zafirah! Desmond!" she shouted. "We need to restrain him!"

The Sages moved into action. Zafirah's hands plunged into the concrete floor, and massive roots erupted from the ground, wrapping themselves around Legion's limbs. Desmond unleashed a barrage of *Malchut* strikes on the chains, breaking them and knocking them away.

Leah saw the ethereal core pulsing with light at the center of Legion's chest. The chains around it had loosened slightly but still maintained their grip.

This is our chance, Asmodeus's voice resonated in her mind. *We must act now!*

Leah nodded, reaching deep within and simultaneously calling on multiple wells of power. *Nehemoth*'s familiar darkness coiled around her arms, stirring something new in her throat.

Gamaliel, Asmodeus whispered. *The Black Speech you used in the alley.*

"Everyone, give it everything you've got!" Helen's voice rang out. "This ends now!"

Leah lunged forward, her hands closing around the ethereal core. Agony lanced through her body the moment she touched it. She screamed as raw energy coursed through her veins. She gritted her teeth and refused to let go.

"Release!" she screamed, her voice distorted by *Gamaliel*'s power.

Black threads of energy erupted from her mouth, wrapping themselves around the core. They twined with the tendrils of *Nehemoth* extending from her arms, creating a web that fought against Legion's chains.

For a moment, nothing happened. Then Micah's knees buckled, his ancient frame no longer able to maintain the freeze. Legion's form shuddered, beginning to break free of *Binah*'s hold.

"Now, Leah!" Helen screamed, blood streaming from her nose as she maintained her position. "We won't get another chance!"

Leah redoubled her efforts, drawing on every scrap of strength she had left. She thought of Eli's sacrifice, her Squares lying injured back at camp, and all the lives Legion had destroyed. The first chain cracked with a sound like shattering glass.

"It's working!" Zafirah shouted, her voice strained as she poured more power into the roots holding Legion.

With a primal scream, Leah gave one final, desperate pull.

Leah's hands trembled as she fell back, clutching the ethereal core. Bright light pulsed off it, illuminating Legion's hovering form over her.

"No," Legion whispered as cracks formed on his face. A

clawed hand reached out for Leah, but before it reached her, it crumbled to ash.

The rest of Legion followed suit, crumbling into nothing.

And in the last seconds of Legion's life, Leah heard Cora whisper, "You would have made a great Immortal Witch."

Then, along with Legion, Leah felt Cora fade away.

CHAPTER 40
THE SCROLL

"She did it!" Sarah's voice rang out in triumph. Around the warehouse, exhausted cheers erupted from the surviving Mystics.

"Leah, are you alright?" Isaac called, starting toward her. Leah spotted Jaime and Jan Xie already moving to help the Knights take down the last of the demons while Zafirah helped support an aged and weakened Micah.

Leah could hardly believe they'd done it—they'd actually killed Legion.

"We did it," she whispered. "It's over."

Leah looked at the core, mesmerized by its swirling patterns, like stardust caught in a glass sphere. Everything else vanished. Her pain. Her exhaustion.

A sharp sting in her palm jolted her back to reality. The eye embedded there by the Librarian blinked open, its pupil contracting as it fixed its unnerving gaze on her.

"Right," Leah muttered. "The scroll."

She scanned the space around her, noting the Knights finishing off the last possessed Mystics. Through it all, she needed to find Helen. She'd know what to do next. She'd know how to contain the core and retrieve the scroll safely.

But as Leah looked across the debris-littered floor, she froze.

Helen lay crumpled on the ground not far away, her pristine white clothing stained with blood. The Queen's body convulsed, the dark liquid seeping from her eyes, nose, and ears.

"Helen!" Leah called out, her heart racing. She stumbled forward; the core still clutched tightly to her chest.

"Leah, wait!" Desmond shouted. "Something's wrong—"

But before anyone could reach her, something impossible happened. Helen glowed a bright golden color, and familiar symbols flared around her. Then bright golden chains erupted from Helen's chest, snaking through the air with terrifying speed.

"No," Leah breathed, recalling the same symbols from the library.

The chains lashed out, wrapping around the core in Leah's hands. She cried out as they seared her skin, trying desperately to maintain her grip.

Don't let go! Asmodeus's voice thundered in her mind. *She's... She's betrayed us!*

"Queen Helen, stop!" Zafirah screamed, launching herself forward with flames erupting from her hands. Without even looking, Helen flicked her wrist. Zafirah froze mid-leap, caught in a powerful *Hod* hold. Desmond tried to circle, but a burst of *Malchut* sent him flying into a support beam.

"Stay back," Helen commanded, her voice resonating with new power. Jan Xie and Jaime moved to attack together, but Helen's golden chains whipped out, forcing them to dodge backward.

Leah strained, fighting against the pull of the chains with every ounce of strength she had left. But her wells were depleted, her body pushed far beyond its limits.

"Helen, stop!" she shouted in a cracked voice. "What are you doing?"

The Queen's eyes snapped open, no longer filled with pain but blazing with triumphant power. With another wave of her hand, she created a barrier of force that kept the other Mystics at bay.

"What I must," Helen replied.

More chains burst forth, coiling around Leah's arms and torso. She screamed as they burned through her clothing, searing her flesh. She saw Desmond trying to break through Helen's barrier through tear-blurred eyes, but even his invulnerability couldn't penetrate it.

The core slipped from her grasp and pulled inexorably toward Helen's waiting hands.

"No!" Leah cried out, desperation clawing at her throat. "What you're doing?"

Helen laughed. "I'm sorry, Leah." She gracefully rose to her feet.

The core hovered between them for a heartbeat, suspended by the competing forces of Leah's fading grip and Helen's golden chains. Then, with a last surge of power, it was wrenched from Leah's hands.

Leah stumbled backward, watching in horror as the core was drawn into Helen's chest. The glowing symbols on the Queen's skin pulsed with blinding intensity, absorbing the core.

Helen's skin glowed a bright golden hue, and all her wounds closed.

"You used me," Leah whispered, the full weight of the betrayal crashing down on her. "All of this time. You knew about the core. And you just wanted it for yourself."

Helen shook her head. "For myself? A demon contained

one of the most powerful things in this universe. Leah, I did this for us. I did this for the future of Mystics. For the future of humanity."

The Queen's clothing mended itself, wrapping her in a pristine black Queens uniform that quickly turned white.

"I couldn't extract the core myself," Helen said. "The scroll's power and my own would have torn me apart. But you…" She fixed Leah with a predatory stare. "You were the perfect conduit. Your connection to your mother, to the Trees of Life and Death… you made it possible."

Leah's mind reeled, pieces falling into place with sickening clarity. "The boxing match," she said. "The attack on the camp. You orchestrated all of it."

Helen nodded. "I needed you isolated, desperate. Willing to take risks."

Rage boiled up inside Leah. "It's been longer than that, hasn't it? How long have you been planning this?" Leah lunged forward, hands outstretched, ready to tear Helen apart with her bare hands if necessary.

But an invisible force slammed into her before she could reach the Queen. Leah crashed to the ground.

"Now, now," Helen said. "There's no need for that. You've played your part. It's time for you to witness the dawn of a new era."

"Get away from her!" Sarah's voice rang out. Leah turned to see her friend charging forward, flames erupting from her hands. Isaac was behind her, his eyes blazing yellow as he prepared to strike.

Jan Xie appeared in a burst of speed, her power flaring. "Helen, what have you done?"

"Stand down," Helen said calmly, raising one hand. Golden light pulsed from her chest, and all three were thrown backward, crashing into the debris-strewn floor.

Zafirah and Desmond rushed to help, but Helen's power held them at bay.

"Your loyalty is admirable," Helen said, her voice resonating with newfound power. "But unnecessary. Everything I do, I do for all of us." The Queen raised her arms. The symbols on her skin blazed like molten gold. "Kneel."

To Leah's horror, she felt her body responding against her will. Her legs buckled, forcing her to her knees. Around the warehouse, she saw others—Mystics, Sages, even the corrupted followers of Legion—all compelled to bow before Helen.

"What have you done?" Leah choked out, fighting against the invisible force pressing down on her.

Helen's eyes shone with inner light as she surveyed the kneeling figures. "I have become your King," she declared. "I am the scroll incarnate. The power to reshape reality itself flows through my veins."

She turned her gaze back to Leah, but before she could speak, Leah's hand burned as the eye in her palm split open.

CHAPTER 41

THREE-FOLD

The eye in Leah's palm burned as it flared to life, its pupil dilating unnaturally. A wave of vertigo washed over her as reality warped and twisted. When the world stopped spinning, she found herself standing in the cavernous expanse of the library.

The Librarian loomed before her, its many eyes blinking in unsettling unison. "Leah Ackerman," it intoned, voice resonating from everywhere at once. "You have failed to uphold our bargain."

Leah's heart raced. "Wait," she pleaded, her voice cracking. "I still have time. Helen, she—"

The Librarian's form rippled, growing larger. "Time has run out. The scroll remains beyond these walls, and now you must pay the price."

Before Leah could argue further, two flashes of light erupted beside her. Her stomach dropped as Sarah and Isaac materialized, their expressions dazed and confused.

"Leah?" Sarah's eyes darted around wildly. "What the hell is going on?"

Isaac stumbled, steadying himself against a nearby shelf. "We're back at the library?"

The Librarian's many arms gestured expansively. "Welcome to your new home. Eternity stretches before you, an endless sea of knowledge to catalog and maintain."

"No," Leah muttered. "They weren't part of the deal. This is between us!"

"Your failure condemns them as well," the Librarian declared. "The debt must be paid threefold for the theft of such precious knowledge."

Sarah's eyes blazed. "Like hell we're staying here!"

The Librarian's form shifted and stretched, pale arms grabbing onto the shelves above them like a spider peering down at its prey. "There is no escape. Your fates are sealed."

Leah couldn't let her friends suffer. Desperately, she reached for her connection to the Trees, hoping to find some well of power that might save them. But the familiar energy slipped through her grasp like smoke.

No! No! No! Asmodeus's voice thundered in her mind. *We can't be trapped here. Not while that core exists!*

Leah felt a surge of energy coursing through her veins. The green flames of *Satariel* erupted around her body, and suddenly, she was in two places at once. One version of herself remained rooted in the library, while another materialized back at the Silos.

The Librarian's many eyes widened in surprise. "Impossible," it breathed. "You shouldn't be able to use *Satariel*. A Well that high in the Tree of Death should kill a mortal in seconds."

Leah looked at her friends for a moment, but before the Librarian could react, the version of her in the library vanished.

She gasped, her vision returning as she stood on an empty battlefield where they had just fought Legion. But something was wrong. It was warmer, and the sun hung lower in the sky than it should, casting long shadows through the hole in the roof. Where there had been fresh debris and scorched earth, nature had already begun to reclaim the space. Dandelions and wildflowers pushed through cracks in the concrete as if a battle hadn't just happened here.

"No," Leah whispered, her voice raw. She spun in a circle, desperately searching for any sign of Sarah or Isaac. "No, no, no!"

The eye in her palm pulsed, and the Librarian's voice echoed in her mind. "Your clever trick may have freed you, but your friends remain mine. Their fates are sealed unless..."

Leah's fists clenched at her sides. "Unless what? Tell me!"

"The scroll must be returned," the Librarian's voice reverberated through her skull. "But it has become one with Helen Nielsen. To free your friends, you must end her life and bring me what remains."

"You... you want me to kill Helen? But no. There must be another way!"

"There is not." The Librarian's tone was final. "Helen Nielsen has become the scroll incarnate. Her death is the only path to your friends' freedom."

She knelt on the concrete, tears streaming down her cheeks. She'd stopped Legion but somehow made things worse. And now, the only way to save her friends was to murder the woman who had guided her for so long.

"How?" she whispered, her voice breaking. "How am I supposed to do this?"

But the Librarian offered no further guidance, the eye sinking back into her palm.

Leah, Asmodeus's voice was uncharacteristically gentle. *We're not safe here. If we're going to save your friends, we need to move.*

She took a shuddering breath, forcing herself to focus. Asmodeus was right. Sarah and Isaac were counting on her. She couldn't fall apart now, no matter how much she wanted to.

Slowly, Leah pushed herself to her feet. She wiped the tears from her face, leaving streaks of dirt and blood across her cheeks. Her gaze swept across the transformed battlefield one last time before settling on the horizon.

"I'm coming, my Queen," Leah murmured, a steel entering her voice that hadn't been there before. "I'll get them back, even if I have to tear down everything you built to do it."

A Small Request From Us, The Authors

Thank you for continuing Leah's journey. We hope you've enjoyed it, so far.

As independent authors, reviews are so important to spread the word and reach new readers.

If you have a few seconds to spare, would you please consider leaving an honest review on the website you bought this book?

Your support helps so much in continuing Leah's story and the many others we plan to write in this world.

All the best,

A.B. Cohen & JP Rindfleisch IX

DIVINE KING
LEAH ACKERMAN SERIES BOOK SIX

The story continues:

https://abcohenwrites.com/divine-king

THE ASTRAL LAYERS
SHORT STORY

Go beyond Leah Ackerman

Delve into a secret world, an impending alliance, and a common enemy. From the shared universe of the Leah Ackerman series, check out this short story now!

https://BookHip.com/QQTLNDW

CURSED JADE
AN ERIC MIZRAHI NOVELETTE

Get it free using the link below:

https://abcohenwrites.com/cursed-jade

ACKNOWLEDGMENTS

This one goes out to our partners, Raquel and Josh. You've been with us since the inception of this series, sticking through our many Sunday meetings, odd ideas, and even stranger writing schedules. It takes a special kind of heart to be with an author, so thank you both—we couldn't have done this without your unwavering support.

A special shout-out to our incredible editor, Zach Bohannon; our beta readers, Chris, Claudia, and Nissim; and our amazing cover designers at Getcovers.com. Your dedication and ongoing efforts have been instrumental in bringing Leah Ackerman's story to life.

And finally, to you—our amazing readers. Thank you for embarking on this journey with us. We hope you've enjoyed *Dire Queen* as much as we've enjoyed writing it, and we can't wait for you to see what comes next in *Divine King*, the sixth and final book of the Leah Ackerman series!

Thank you all.

A.B. Cohen & JP Rindfleisch IX

About the Authors

A.B. Cohen is an author of freaky stories for weird people. He focus mainly on thrillers, horror and urban fantasy tales. Originally from Caracas, Venezuela, today he lives in San Francisco, California. Along with his passion for writing, he also loves dancing, soccer, and traveling. You can find out more about A.B. Cohen's upcoming writing projects using the link below:

www.abcohenwrites.com

JP Rindfleisch IX is a horror, urban fantasy, and science fiction writer. They live in Rockford, Illinois, with their partner of eleven years, and a menagerie of animal children including a Siberian husky, miniature dachshund, African grey parrot, Quaker parrot, and a run of the mill cat. They love creating art, nerding out over science, video games, tabletop RPGs, and spending hours in the kitchen crafting delectable vegan grub. You can learn more about JP Rindfleisch IX by following the link below:

www.jprindfleischix.com

www.ingramcontent.com/pod-product-compliance
Lightning Source LLC
Chambersburg PA
CBHW061123310726
48974CB00002B/654